Hockey Night in Transcona

John Danakas

James Lorimer & Company, Publishers
Toronto, 1995

James Lorimer & Company Ltd. acknowledges with thanks the support of the Canada Council, the Ontario Arts Council, and the Ontario Publishing Centre in the development of writing and publishing in Canada.

Cover illustration: Daniel Shelton

Canada Cataloguing in Publication Data

John Danakas
    Hockey Night in Transcona

(Sports stories)
ISBN 1-55028-505-X (bound). – ISBN 1-55028-504-1 (pbk.)

I. Title.   II. Series: Sports stories (Toronto, Ont.)

PS8557.A53H6 1995	jC813'.54	C95–
932461–5		
PZ7.D35Ho 1995		

James Lorimer & Company, Limited
35 Britain Street
Toronto, Ontario
M5A 1R7

Printed and bound in Canada

Contents

This book is dedicated to the many wonderful teachers, librarians, and especially students whom I have met in schools across Manitoba over the last three years. Thanks.

1

Stars on Ice

Cody Powell picked up the puck off the boards at centre ice and flew towards the opposing net. His skates pumped hard, shooting ice shavings into the cold air, and his stick handled the puck expertly, as if the puck were somehow magnetized to the blade. Beneath his blue and red Jets jersey, his heart pounded with the excitement of the goal he could sense he was about to score.

At the blue line, Cody spied a defender looming tall in a yellow Penguins jersey — Ryan Miller. Instantly deciding to try a deke play, Cody sliced the blades of his skates sideways into the ice, came to a split-second stop directly in front of Ryan, twirled around in a tight backward arc, the puck still on his stick, and took off in the opposite direction, leaving Ryan with his legs tied up in a knot.

This is going to be a play for the highlight tapes, Cody thought, smiling to himself. He swayed his hips from side to side, once again building up momentum, and in a second came face-to-face with the goaltender, Ernie Gaines, who had slid out of his crease to challenge Cody. Cody faked to the left with his shoulders, then poked the puck with his stick to the right, sending Ernie sprawling onto the ice face-first, lifting his glove in a last-ditch effort to make a save.

Cody measured up the puck on his backhand and with the force of his powerful wrists raised the puck towards the net.

The puck zoomed past Ernie's outstretched glove and crossed the line.

A goal!

As his teammate, Mitch Porter, patted him on the back, Cody threw up his arms in celebration. Closing his eyes tightly, he could almost feel the applause of the fans wash over his body.

Meanwhile, Ernie kicked his goalpost in frustration, sending up a tinny clang that jarred Cody from his reverie.

In an instant, Cody was no longer in Winnipeg Arena, having just scored a picture-perfect goal in front of a crowd of thousands of cheering fans. He wasn't even, he admitted to himself, in Lord Strathcona Arena winning a game for the Transcona Sharks in their twelve-year-olds' community club league. Those were mere fantasies. No, he was on a crummy outdoor rink two blocks from his home, and the only sound in the air other than the reverberating clang from the kicked goalpost — which was actually an aluminum garbage can dragged onto the ice from the adjacent back lane — was the clatter of train cars switching tracks at the nearby CN railyard.

"I'm freezing my butt off," Ernie grunted as he retrieved the puck and slid back to the other boys. Ernie was wearing winter boots. Playing goalie all the time, he'd never learned to skate. "Can we call it quits already?"

"Yeah, let's get going," Mitch agreed. His breath turned to vapour in the cold December air. "I have some math homework to do."

The four boys were using only half the ice surface of the outdoor rink. They had a net set up along the centre line — Cody and Mitch's goal — and two garbage cans — Ryan and Ernie's goal — in front of the rickety boards at the end facing the CN yard.

"It *is* getting kind of late," Cody put in, figuring maybe it was best to just go home. As much as he loved playing hockey, what was the use playing two-on-two pickup games all the time? The Transcona Sharks, in their official turquoise and grey uniforms with the players' numbers and names printed across the backs, were the real thing. They hosted games in their own arena and travelled across the city and even the province to play other community club teams. They had been the City East runners-up last year. If only his mother were willing to put up with the cost of letting him sign up! But she wasn't. She kept reminding Cody that there was only so much money to go around now that she and his dad had divorced. Cody whacked his stick against the ice at the thought. It just wasn't fair.

Just then Ryan skated back to the other boys, joining them in a huddle around Ernie and his garbage-can goalpost.

"Let's play just a little longer," Ryan begged, even though he lived farthest from the rink, in a new house in the east end of Transcona. "I'm still having fun." His parents wouldn't let him play organized hockey, either. They had a different reason than Cody's mom, though: they were afraid their son might get injured. As a result, Ryan also had to satisfy himself with these after-school pickup games, which, at his parents' insistence, he played wearing all the necessary equipment.

"But I can hardly see the puck it's so dark," Mitch whined.

"Next goal wins, then," Ryan suggested, readjusting his shoulder pads. Tall and thin as a rail, he was always making sure his equipment was on right. Cody had a feeling Ryan was just as afraid of injuring himself as his parents were.

"You've got to be kidding!" Mitch answered. "The score's thirty-three to twenty-six. We're ahead by seven goals."

Sometimes it seemed to Cody that what Mitch enjoyed most about these games was keeping score. He'd make a great sportscaster someday, that was for sure.

"So what?" Ryan retorted. "You want to get home fast, right? Well, it shouldn't take too long to score one goal."

"Next goal wins, huh?" As Cody repeated Ryan's suggestion, he took off his toque and ran a hand through his brown hair. It might be fun to play under pressure, he thought, just like the pros and the Transcona Sharks in their important league games. "You're on!" The pinpoint freckles around his nose danced as his mouth formed a smile.

The two pairs of boys retreated to their ends of the rink to plot their sudden-death overtime strategies. Cody took off his battered and faded old hockey gloves, jammed them between his legs, and traced the pattern of the play he was planning on the palm of his hand. Knowing Mitch would much rather be at home right now in the warm comfort of his room, arranging his collection of sports cards — which included three Eric Lindros rookies and an Edmonton Oiler Wayne Gretzky — Cody tried to make the play as simple as possible. Mitch wiped his fogged-up glasses with a tissue he had pulled out of his parka pocket and took a close look.

"If I win the face-off," Cody explained, "you move forward to pick up the puck and I'll skate wide right. Then you pass to me and head to the net." He was pretty confident he'd win the draw. His dad had taught him a trick where he held the stick backwards with his left hand and pulled at the puck rather than poking it.

"If we lose the face-off?" Mitch retied the hood of his parka over his head to warm his chilled ears.

"Get back into net as fast as you can and I'll backtrack to intercept the man with the puck." Cody straightened his back. He was of average height and weight, with an athletic build.

"Got it," Mitch said.

The boys took their positions: Cody and Ryan poised for the face-off, Mitch and Ernie hanging back on defence, ready to turn into goaltenders if the puck moved towards them, or into forwards if their teammates controlled the puck up ice.

A north wind blew suddenly across the ice and stung Cody's face. What I wouldn't give to be able to play in an indoor arena, he thought again.

With no referee to drop the puck, Cody and Ryan simply placed the blades of their sticks flat on the ice, the puck in the spot dead centre between the two blades. Then they raised their sticks and knocked them against each other. Once, ready. Twice, set. And three to …

The face-off never happened. Just as Cody and Ryan were about to jam away at the free puck, a series of booming noises echoed over the rink, and the two boys, as well as Mitch and Ernie, turned their heads to see what the commotion was all about.

A fleet of cars and minivans had driven up to the outdoor rink and all the noise came from doors swinging open or slamming shut. Cody stood motionless in the bright glow of the headlights, as a stream of kids piled out of the vehicles and strode towards the rink, their skates slung across their sticks.

Cody couldn't believe his eyes. As the kids approached the ice, he could make out that most of them were wearing the turquoise and grey uniform of the Transcona Sharks, with the stick-chomping shark emblazoned on the front of their chests.

"Hurry up, men!" an adult male voice bellowed from behind the trunk of one of the cars. "Let's get this tryout practice started."

In a moment Cody could hear the man's boots crunching over the gravel path leading to the rink. He was wearing a Sharks jacket, the title "Coach" sewn across the right arm. Cody recognized the man as Mr. Brackett, the father of one of his classmates, Stu Brackett. Word around school was that Mr. Brackett had once played junior hockey with a team in Alberta. To hear Stu tell the story, Mr. Brackett would have made it to the NHL if only he hadn't seriously injured his right knee.

"This isn't an ideal ice surface, but it'll have to do." Mr. Brackett sliced some chipped ice off the rink with the blade of his stick and flung it contemptuously over the boards into the surrounding snow. "I wish someone had told me the fifteen-year-olds had booked Lord Strathcona Arena tonight."

He stepped away from the rink and with a key opened the metal power box on the outside wall of the changing shack. He turned on the rink's lights and the ice surface seemed suddenly brilliant beneath their yellow glare.

"I wasn't too sure those old lights would work," he said. "I think they date back to prehistoric times."

By now at least a half-dozen of the boys on the team had laced on their skates and jumped over the boards onto the ice. Two pairs of players hauled mesh nets with red steel goalposts onto the rink, while another, slender and brown-haired — Cody recognized him as Stu Brackett — emptied a canvas bag full of pucks onto the ice. Hard, official pucks, not spongees like Cody and the boys used. The Sharks players each gathered up a puck and skated around the rink working on their stickhandling, entirely ignoring the fact that other players were on the ice right now. They seemed to expect the boys to automatically slink off and make way for them.

Cody, Ryan, Ernie, and Mitch stood in quiet shock and amazement at their end of the rink. More and more Sharks players hurdled the wooden boards, like an invading army in one of the old war movies Cody used to watch with his dad. Soon the four boys were surrounded by a sea of fast-moving turquoise and grey jerseys. Cody felt, suddenly, as if he and his friends were somehow in the way. But this was *their* rink, where the boys played each day after school and on Saturday mornings, too. They couldn't just give it up. But what exactly were they to do?

At the same time, Cody couldn't help admiring the Sharks players. They glided across the ice in smooth strides and made precise passes that echoed loudly in the night air. What a team! Cody would have given anything to be able to play with them.

"We were here first!" Ernie muttered to his buddies. "I say we don't budge until we're good and ready."

Ryan couldn't help chuckling. "A few minutes ago you were so cold you wanted to run straight home."

"Well, I'm not cold anymore," Ernie said. In the next instant, he intercepted a pass from one of the Sharks players that was aimed across ice and cleared the puck to the far boards. "We were here first," he snarled, loud enough for a few of the Sharks to hear him.

"Hey, what's the idea?" the Sharks player who now had to chase down the puck called out. His red hair flowed out from behind his helmet. "We're trying to practise here, you know!"

"And we're trying to play!" Ernie answered back. His round black face was fierce.

The Sharks player snickered. "You might want to go home then and pick up your skates," he taunted. "That's if you own any, of course." Before Ernie or anybody else could think of a reply, the player skated away in a flash.

Cody felt bad for Ernie. Even though Ernie couldn't skate, Cody knew how good a goalie he was. He rarely lost sight of the puck and possessed great reflexes. In fact, he loved goaltending so much he'd scouted garage sales across the city with his mother last spring to pick up all the goalie equipment he needed. Cody wished he could show these Sharks that he and his friends were no slouches when it came to hockey.

In the next moment, without thinking, Cody raced to the pile of loose pucks at centre ice and, snatching one with his stick, streaked down the left wing towards the far net. As Cody picked up steam, the Sharks player who'd just insulted Ernie emerged to defend the net. The player tried to squeeze Cody away from centre ice and into the boards. But Cody kept his head up and deftly slipped the puck between the defender's legs. Then he slithered past the player, like someone sneaking through a door about to be closed in his face, stretched out his stick with his right hand to pick up the puck, and rocketed towards the goalie. The heavier weight of the hard puck on the blade of his stick sent a thrill through his arms. With a quick flick of his wrists, he drilled the puck into the upper right-hand corner of the net, just over the goalie's glove.

Cody looked back at his buddies. They were cheering wildly. He smiled. Then he turned to the Sharks player. "Ernie would have stopped that one," he remarked quietly.

The Sharks player was silent at first. Then he opened his mouth. "Nice play," he said. "But real league hockey's a lot different from the shinny you guys play."

"Not too different, I bet," Cody commented. Inside he was hoping word would get around the Sharks team that he was a player they could really use.

By then Mr. Brackett had come onto the ice, standing tall in an expensive-looking pair of skates and long black hockey pants with a white stripe down the side. "I'd ask you boys to join us," he began, looking over Cody, Ryan, Mitch, and Ernie, "but you're not properly equipped." Cody noticed the coach roll his eyes at the sight of his old gloves and moved them behind his back. "You're certainly welcome to stay and watch, though."

"Thanks, but no thanks," Ernie shot back.

"It's up to you, boys," Mr. Brackett said, forcing out a smile. "But this is our second-to-last tryout and we have to get cracking. The season begins in two weeks and I need to have chosen a full squad by then." With that he shoved out a leg and skated to the other end of the rink, where a bunch of players were working on their wrist shots.

Cody couldn't help thinking that he'd give almost anything to have a chance to impress this coach. He belonged on the Transcona Sharks.

"Let's get out of here," Mitch suggested. "Who needs the fuss?"

"I'd like to stay and watch," Cody cut in. "I mean, this is a real league team tryout. I think it'll be interesting. We might even learn something."

"Not," Ernie mumbled.

"Maybe Cody's right," Ryan said. "I wouldn't mind watching a real hockey practice."

"Naw, I'm going home," Ernie said.

"Me too," Mitch dittoed.

After Ernie and Mitch had left, Cody and Ryan skated off the ice and tramped through the hard-packed snow around the rink to a spot just outside the boards at centre ice. Their skates left narrow crisscross slashes in the snow. Cody pulled his toque farther down over his ears and loosened the laces on his skates to relax his ankles. Ryan took off his helmet and propped it on the butt of his stick. In the distance smoke billowed out of the CN shops smokestack.

"I wish Mr. Brackett would lend us that key to the power box," Ryan said. "If we could turn on the lights ourselves, we could play all the way to bedtime."

Cody shook his head from side to side. "But it still wouldn't be an indoor arena, and we still wouldn't be playing for a league team."

"Tell me about it," Ryan said. "Look at those guys out there. Now that's real hockey."

Cody didn't need any encouragement to watch every move the Sharks players were making out on the ice. They moved in geometric patterns, their equipped bodies and helmeted faces making them look almost like professionals. They skated on one foot and then the other, they sprinted from end to end, they guided themselves around bright orange pylons set in a line running the length of the rink. This was a genuine hockey practice.

At one point Mr. Brackett had all the Sharks players line up at one end of the rink, their backs to the far end, their sticks slung across their shoulders.

"Now I want you all to skate backwards to the other end of the rink," he commanded.

The players waited tensely.

"On your marks, get set ..." At that, he pulled out a metal whistle and sent a shrill note tearing through the cold night air. The players pushed off, their legs working hard against the ice. To Cody, the drill resembled running through water at the beach. Only backwards!

As the players back-skated down the ice, Mr. Brackett skated along with them, facing the players, while all the time barking out comments. His face was red with excitement and his black brush moustache seemed to bristle.

"A little harder!"

"That's too slow!"

"Do you guys want to make the Sharks or are you going to settle for the B squad?"

"Last one there has to skate five laps!"

By the time the players had reached the other end, they seemed exhausted. But none of them dared collapse onto the ice. They stood waiting at attention for Mr. Brackett to call out the next drill.

"Wow," Ryan commented. "That coach really tears into the kids."

"This is league hockey, remember," Cody said, keeping his eyes on the Sharks players. In his mind he was seeing himself out there, confident he would be able to keep pace. "There's no fooling around."

The Transcona Sharks played in games that meant something, Cody reminded himself. There were standings and playoffs and trophies to think of. And Cody was thinking of just those things right now.

He wanted a chance to play on the Transcona Sharks. More than anything else in the world.

In the night sky, a full moon sat perched, like some sort of crystal ball. Cody looked up at it with hopeful eyes.

Come to think of it, he told himself, maybe he hadn't pestered his mom enough about letting him sign up for the team. Tomorrow after school, when he'd had time to come up with a new approach, he'd ask his mom one final time.

This time, she had better say yes.

2

Little House on the Prairie

"Is Mom home from work yet, Tish?" Cody called out to his sister, Letisha, as he plunked down his school books on the kitchen table.

"No." Tish's head didn't move from in front of the television set. Glancing at the screen, Cody knew instantly that she was watching yet another episode of *Little House on the Prairie*. There was no interrupting her until the show was over and she'd cried herself out long and hard. The things a seven-year-old girl will do for a good time, Cody thought, shaking his head.

He opened the fridge door and peered inside. Slim pickings. Ever since his dad had moved out over a year ago, his mom, it seemed, had stopped stocking the fridge with anything that tasted good. Fruit and vegetables had replaced cake and cold cuts. He settled for a glass of chocolate milk and sat down to consider the best way to persuade his mom to let him sign up for league hockey. The longer he considered, the more he realized his chances were not very good. He knew his mom. When she made a decision, she usually stuck by it.

In a few minutes, Tish's show was over and she zapped off the television with the remote. She entered the cramped kitchen. Immediately, she arranged Cody's books into a neat pile and pulled a coaster out of a cabinet to place under his glass.

"Do you have to?" Cody sneered, gulping down the last of his milk. "I'm trying to think."

"I like to keep things in order around here," Tish protested. She pushed shut the spout of the milk carton and replaced it in the fridge. "Mom's so tired from work all the time and you're such a slob, so somebody has to." She smiled warmly. "But I don't mind."

Cody rolled his eyes. Since his parents' divorce, Tish had developed an obsession about keeping the house in order. He wished she'd lay off. Right now all he wanted to think about was finding a way to join the Transcona Sharks.

"What's the problem?" Tish asked. Her blonde braids jiggled. "Maybe I can help?"

"That's unlikely," Cody said. "Unless you know of an instant way to come up with three hundred dollars or so." He walked to the pantry and dug himself a huge handful of cereal from out of a box.

"I think I do," Tish said.

Cody didn't say anything right away because he was still munching the dry cereal. The second he'd swallowed, he made his crack. "And what are they teaching kids in grade two nowadays, how to rob banks? I don't think I remember that unit. Would that be in social studies or science?" He moved to the couch and started channel surfing with the remote.

Tish followed Cody to the living room and took a seat next to him on the couch.

"I think you should call up Dad and ask him for the money, as a Christmas gift," Tish said.

"Yeah, right," Cody muttered. The last thing he wanted right now was to be reminded of his dad. From the moment he'd heard, just before the school year started, that his dad was moving with a whole new family to Kamloops, British Columbia, Cody'd decided he was no longer talking to him. He had learned to accept the idea of his parents living apart, but this was too much. Why'd his dad have to get remarried and move out of town? Now he had two new kids. As far as Cody was concerned, his dad was a traitor.

"Why don't you give him a chance?" Tish pleaded with Cody. She was hugging a pink throw pillow close to her chest. Her green eyes, still faintly moist from watching the show, were looking straight into his.

"Because he doesn't deserve one." Cody's throat caught, and he could feel his stomach knot. He remembered the times he'd practised stickhandling moves with his dad in the tiny rink they had created in the back yard by flooding the area between the driveway and the neighbour's fence. The two of them would probably never do that again. "In case you didn't notice, Tish, he has another family now."

Tish's face was red, and Cody could see her trying to hold back tears. It's funny, he thought, how easily she cries at her TV shows, but how good she is at fighting back tears when it comes to our own family's problems.

"But Dad promised to keep loving us," Tish went on. "He's still our dad. I'm sure he'll want to help you."

"It doesn't matter anyway," Cody said. "I'm not talking to him, so I guess that means I can't ask him."

"Well, I will then," Tish said. "I'm writing him a letter tonight, telling him what I want for Christmas. I'll tell him what you want, too. He'll take care of it, Cody. You'll see."

Cody flung the remote onto the couch behind him and started stomping towards his bedroom, which he shared with Tish. "Don't you dare," he said, scowling.

When he'd entered the bedroom, he slammed the door behind him. He picked up a hockey magazine from underneath his bed and lay down to read it. But he couldn't concentrate on the words or even the pictures. Right now his mind was full of other things. Too many other things, he decided, when all he really wanted to think about was one thing: trying out for the Transcona Sharks.

Outside a gust of wind howled and Cody felt the bedroom wall rattle a moment from its force.

About a half-hour later, Cody heard his mom opening the back door. Enough moping around, he thought, it's time to take care of business. He jumped out of bed and ran to greet her.

"Mom, how you doing?" he called out, as his mom kicked off her boots. He reached for her lunch pail. "Let me help you with that."

As he took it, he stepped by mistake into a little puddle of melting snow. Right now he couldn't care less.

"How was work, Mom?" Cody decided to go for broke and really lay on the nice-guy treatment.

His mom rubbed her temples with her hands and took a deep breath. "Don't ask. Rumour around the shop is that one hundred of us are going to be laid off next month. One hundred! I'm so low on the seniority list, I know I'll be one of them."

Just great, Cody thought disappointedly. I picked the perfect day to ask for an extra three hundred dollars of allowance money.

"Mom," Tish called out from the kitchen. "Can I get supper started? I took that pickerel out of the freezer this morning like you asked me."

"I'll help," Cody added. Tish's eyes popped wide open. He glared back at her. "You just sit down and relax, Mom. I'm sure you've had a hard day."

Cody's mom grinned. "Hold on here for a moment." She hung up her parka and started walking to the kitchen. "Tish, I'm used to seeing you so eager to cook supper. You, Cody, I'm not. Your idea of helping with supper is volunteering to pick up the phone to order pizza. What's the occasion?"

Cody tried hard to put on his very best innocent-little-boy face. It was a long shot, but Cody could remember a few times it had worked wonders for him.

"Nothing, Mom. I just want to help."

"Sure, sure." Cody's mom glanced through the day's mail. "Out with it, Cody. What's it this time? Your teacher wants to talk to me about your math marks? Or do you want to spend the weekend sleeping over at Ryan's house again?"

"No, Mom," Cody answered. "It's nothing like that." He could feel the nervousness working inside him like a sore stomach.

Cody's mom washed her hands at the kitchen sink. Then she took the pickerel out of its plastic bag and placed it on a metal plate. At the same time, Tish pulled vegetables out of the fridge to make a salad. Cody did his best to help her, taking hold of a head of lettuce.

"Actually, Mom," he began again, starting to chop the lettuce, "what I have to ask you has to do with my future." Cody liked the ring of that.

His mom's eyebrows shot up. "Explain," she commanded.

Cody didn't know where to begin. "Are you sure you don't want to take your bath first, Mom?"

"No," she replied. "Explain."

Cody kept chopping the lettuce. His eyes were on the knife in front of him, not on his mom. "You know how I'd like to be a professional hockey player someday, Mom? Well, in order to receive the right training, I have to ..."

"No, no, and no again." Cody's mom shook her head. "There's no way I'm forking up nearly a thousand dollars so you can play league hockey. There's a rink down the lane, you can play there." She opened a cupboard door and took down a bottle of oil. "League hockey's just too expensive. Come springtime, you can sign up for soccer." She nodded her head meaningfully. "Now that's a sport. All you need are shoes, shorts, and a ball."

"Mom!" Cody pleaded. "It's not that much money. I figure it'll only cost about three hundred dollars."

"Still too much," Cody's mom insisted. "Your sister takes her ballet lessons, you just demanded I buy you two new pairs of jeans, and I did, not to mention the Chicago Bulls jacket I bought you before school started, and I have to pay the mortgage on this house. I'm a single mother, remember, who just might be laid off. Give me a break."

Cody pouted. Something inside him snapped. "Well, maybe if you weren't a single mother, you could afford to sign me up."

"What's that supposed to mean, young man?" Cody's mom had her hands set stiffly on her hips.

Cody stormed towards his room. "It means you and Dad didn't have to get divorced." He could feel the tears burning his eyes.

"Cody Powell, you come back here and speak to me face-to-face," Cody's mom called after him. She rummaged through the drawer where she kept a pack of emergency cigarettes hidden — she'd been trying to quit for over a month now — and pulled one out. "I deserve that much. I am your mom, you know." Cody could detect a catch in her voice. He decided to turn back.

Tish broke in then. "Listen," she said. "I could give up my ballet lessons. I'm not so sure I'll ever be a ballerina."

Cody stood silently facing his mother. She flung a loose strand of hair back over her head, nervously lighted her cigarette, then leaned down to hug Tish.

"That won't be necessary," she said. "We'll come up with a solution."

Cody worked back the tears. "Mom, please, isn't there some way?"

She moved towards him then and took him in her arms. She kissed his cheeks. Cody made a play at pulling away, but admitted to himself that his mother's warmth felt good.

"Cody, I just can't afford to sign you up on the league team." She was looking straight into his eyes. "I don't have that kind of money."

"Please!"

"I'm sorry, Cody."

"I really want to play on a league team, Mom."

"I know you do." She stood up and placed the pickerel in the oven. "But it's too expensive. There's not just the registration costs. There's the equipment, ice fees, tournament fees. Believe me, I know all about it. I had two brothers who were hockey nuts."

"This is all I'll ever ask for."

Cody's mom wiped his face. "I'll tell you what," she said. "Christmas is coming up. How about this Saturday afternoon the three of us go and buy you an early Christmas gift — a new pair of hockey skates."

Cody didn't say anything.

"Not second-hand ones like the ones you have now, but brand new ones."

Still Cody didn't say a word.

"With brand new skates you'll go flying around the ice," his sister added. "You'll be a real Eric What's-His-Name."

Cody couldn't help cracking a smile. He completed the name for his little sister. "Lindros," he said.

Cody's mom smiled. "What do you say?"

"OK," he said. "I'll take the new skates."

His mom hugged him again and he hugged her back.

But inside he knew new skates weren't enough. His mom hadn't pulled through for him, just like his father hadn't pulled through for him when he moved away.

As far as Cody was concerned, he had been let down. Left on his own. Once again. He released himself from his mom, straightened up, and headed to his room.

3

A Meeting at the Igloo

It's final," Cody declared to his friends. "I won't be playing league hockey this year either."

The four boys were gathered after their Saturday morning two-on-two hockey game in a snow fort they'd built in the empty field behind Ernie's house. They'd worked hard over the past two weeks laying down blocks of hard-packed snow and binding them together by pouring on water and letting it freeze. They'd even managed to partially roof the fort's four walls with a sheet of plywood, which they'd camouflaged with snow. The fort was situated behind a stand of tall elm trees, so nobody noticed it unless they knew about it. And the only people who knew about it were the four boys. They referred to their snow fort simply as "the Igloo."

"So your mom didn't budge?" Ryan asked. He bit at his thumb, trying to disengage a sliver lodged there from his hockey stick.

"Zilch." Cody took a sip of hot chocolate from the thermos Ernie always brought to their games. "Except I do get a brand new pair of skates this afternoon as a consolation prize."

"That's not bad," Mitch offered. He was sitting comfortably on one of Ernie's goalie pads with Ryan. Ernie and Cody sat on the other pad.

"But it won't get me on the Sharks," Cody said.

"How much money exactly would you need?" Mitch asked.

"I figure three hundred dollars," Cody replied. "One hundred and fifty for the registration and one hundred and fifty for some equipment. And that's a bottom-of-the-line estimate."

"And how about your dad," Ryan queried, still working on his sliver. "Can't he help you?"

"Maybe he could, maybe he couldn't," Cody said matter-of-factly. "But I don't care to ask him."

None of the boys pursued the issue.

Mitch scratched his head. "You know," he began, "if I traded in some of my cards — that 1987–88 Topps Edmonton Oiler Wayne Gretzky, for example, and maybe my Teemu Selanne rookie card — I could come up with almost a hundred dollars."

Cody patted Mitch on the shoulder. "Thanks, Mitch, but that wouldn't be right. You keep your collection the way it is. One day it'll be worth millions." Cody picked at a strand of loose tape on his stick. "I guess I can do without the Transcona Sharks for one more year."

"It sure would be something, though," Mitch said, "to see one of us playing with the Sharks."

"I don't think it would be such a big deal," Ernie snapped. He had stood up and with mitted hands was smoothing out the snow on one of the walls of the fort. "From what I saw, those guys on the Sharks are a bunch of snooty jerks."

"And Cody would put them in their place," Mitch retorted. "That's the whole point. I wish he could have a crack at making that team. That would show the Sharks that we're no pushovers."

"Who cares?" Ernie said. "I'm happy just playing on our rink after school."

"But Cody could be a star someday," Mitch offered. "And we can say we knew him when."

"I don't know," Ernie persisted. "That Coach Brackett sure seems like a mean guy."

"I won't argue with that," Ryan agreed. "He really works that team hard."

"Cody can take it," Mitch said.

Not far off a train whistle blew. Right there in "the Igloo" Cody could almost feel the train's wheels chugging down the tracks.

"Let's not argue," Cody said. "I mean, there's no chance I'll be trying out for the Sharks anyhow."

"Well, if you did have a chance, I know you could make the team," Ryan said. "I bet they could use a fancy stickhandler like you to help them score more goals."

"Thanks," Cody said. It felt good having someone compliment him. "You could probably make the team yourself."

"Maybe, if my parents would let me," Ryan agreed. "But the Sharks play pretty rough." Finally he pried the sliver loose. "There it is," he announced, holding up the thin shard of wood. "Anybody have a band-aid?"

Ernie groaned. "Yeah, like I carry one in my back pocket all the time."

"Just checking." Ryan smiled. He was usually pretty good at taking cracks from the guys for being so cautious.

Snow began powdering from the sky. Cody turned his head up to catch some of the wet flakes on his face.

"Let's get going," Ernie said. "If this snow keeps up I'll have a lot of shovelling ahead of me: three driveways and two sidewalks, and that's not including our own, which I'm hoping my dad'll do."

The boys began gathering their things. Sticks, skates, gloves, pucks. In a few moments they were ready to leave.

"Hold on," Ryan said. "I have an idea." Immediately he began unzipping the duffel bag full of his equipment that he'd just closed a second ago.

"What now?" Ernie complained. He was standing lopsidedly on account of his own duffel bag full of goalie equipment slung across his left shoulder. "You forget something?"

"No." Ryan pulled out piece after piece of his hockey equipment and carried it to Cody. "Just bear with me." He held each piece of equipment in turn against Cody's body so that Cody soon resembled someone trying on new clothes in front of a mirror without actually putting them on.

"OK, I get the idea," Mitch said. "You loan your hockey stuff to Cody. I thought of that myself. But that still doesn't get him on the team. What about registration costs?"

"Who said Cody was going to register?" Ryan smiled mischievously. "Next week the Sharks are having their final tryout practice. I heard Mr. Brackett say so myself. Every twelve-year-old who's signed up for league hockey will be there. That must be about fifty kids from all over Transcona. Well, I say Cody should just sneak into that practice wearing my equipment and, of course, the brand new skates his mom buys him this afternoon, and do his thing. So he'll get caught by the end of the practice? By then ..."

Mitch broke in suddenly, "... he'll have proven to the snooty Sharks hot-shots that he's just as good as they are."

"If not better," Ryan put in. He was grinning widely. "And he'll have had, I bet," Ryan looked directly at Cody, "one of the best times of his life."

"A real Cinderella story," Mitch pronounced. There he was being a sportscaster again.

Cody stood dumbfounded. He didn't quite know what to make of Ryan's idea. It sounded good, though. If he couldn't get a whole season of league hockey, he'd be more than willing to settle for a little taste, even if that taste was just a tryout practice.

"That plan," Mitch said, "is just crazy enough that it could work. I can't wait to see the faces of those Sharks players when Cody skates circles around them."

"You guys really want to see this happen, huh?" Ernie asked.

"Yeah," Ryan and Mitch answered.

"I don't get it. I thought we were having fun playing by ourselves."

"We are," Ryan admitted. "But league hockey's different. It's the first step to becoming a professional."

Cody still did not say a word.

Ryan pulled out his red plastic helmet with the metal face guard and fitted it over Cody's head. It was a little big but when Ryan snapped on the chin strap it at least stayed in place. Ryan stood in front of Cody and straightened the helmet as best he could.

"I present to you, ladies and gentlemen," he announced, "the next Transcona Sharks left wing hockey ace, if only for a day: Number 18, Cody Powell."

Mitch clapped his hands wildly and whistled as loudly as he could.

Finally, Cody decided to open his mouth. "You guys are crazy," he said, "but I love the idea." With the sudden movement of his mouth, the chin strap came loose and the helmet tumbled from his head to the ground. Cody couldn't help breaking out in a giggle. All three other boys joined him.

Ernie approached Cody. "I think you're making a mistake," he said, "but if this is what you want, good luck."

"Yeah, this is what I want," Cody said. He wished his parents understood him as well as his friends.

Now Cody picked up the fallen helmet and replaced it on his head. His mind filled with glorious thoughts of playing for the Sharks.

He turned serious again for a moment. "I won't disappoint you, guys," he said. "I promise."

4

Drilled to Death

Cody's body was plastered onto the boards, his helmet knocking once, twice against the Plexiglas. His head seemed to swish around inside the helmet like jello inside a bowl. Then the defender who'd nailed him finished the job off by sneaking a quick elbow to the ribs. A whistle blew. "Way to play physical, Travis!" Coach Brackett called out. "Boys, you can take a break. We'll get back to more drills in a few minutes."

Cody had had no idea a simple tryout practice could be so rough. He straightened himself and closed his eyes for a moment to regain his composure. Then he reopened them. Sure enough, he was still inside Lord Strathcona Arena. No matter how difficult his first league practice was turning out to be, he had to admit that playing in a place like this was a real thrill. He took a long look around. The place was enormous. Colourful banners proclaiming several championships hung from the rafters, and an immense portrait of Lord Strathcona adorned the wall. From history class Cody knew Lord Strathcona was the guy who'd driven in the last spike on Canada's transcontinental railway; the name Transcona was a combination of his name and transcontinental. There was a huge electronic scoreboard under the portrait and a glassed-in observation deck at the near end of the arena, where a bunch of parents were now standing, holding styrofoam cups of coffee and talking among themselves. That's where my dad should be right now, Cody couldn't help thinking. Not out in Kamloops, British Columbia.

At least Ryan, Mitch, and Ernie had come out to support him. Cody turned and glanced their way. They were sitting behind the home bench, not saying much because they didn't want to draw attention to Cody and ruin his cover, but closely watching his every move. He felt better knowing they were there.

Cody wished he could give his friends something to cheer about. They were waiting for him to show up the Sharks players, but so far he'd been the one shown up. All the clutching and grabbing from the other players had thrown him off course. Not to mention that he'd felt awkward and stiff in Ryan's too-loose equipment.

Cody was actually relieved to be wearing his tattered old hockey gloves and Jets jersey. They reminded him of the kind of hockey he was capable of playing. He wished he could display his stickhandling skills sometime soon. Maybe that would make an impression.

As most of the other players sat catching their breath, Cody pushed off with the new skates his mother had just bought him — they needed working in — and glided down the ice. He couldn't get enough of this ice surface. To Cody it seemed as smooth and white as a pool filled with milk. It sure would be nice to call this arena home, Cody thought.

"OK, boys, here's your opportunity to prove you're actually men," Coach Brackett announced just then. "This next drill is called a 'Manmaker,' and for good reason." He seemed to be strutting as he skated to and fro on the ice. "We'll perform this drill in two groups of twenty-five. You all line up on the goal line, then skate to the blue line and back. Then to the centre line and back. And so on, until you've skated to each line on the ice and back." He pulled out his clipboard.

"I'll be identifying those players who finish in the top five in each heat, and I guarantee them a spot on this team."

All fifty players let out a gasp. Here was a chance to earn an automatic spot on the Transcona Sharks. As far as Cody was concerned, registered or not, he was going to make the most of it.

Coach Brackett separated the players into Odds and Evens. Cody was an Even. His heat would be skating last.

The Odds lined up. Cody could see how nervous they all were by the way they fidgeted in place, awaiting Coach Brackett's starting whistle. Inside his own stomach he felt a little flutter.

"On your marks, get set, go!" The whistle blew shrilly inside the cavernous arena.

The players took off like a herd of stampeding buffalo. The drill was definitely difficult. You could see the strain of each movement — the starting and stopping, the hairpin turns, the sprinting — in the soon tired legs of the players and the heaving of their chests.

Cody had a hard time recognizing most of the players beneath their helmets and face guards, but he did notice a couple of guys from his grade seven class. Cody wondered if he had what it took to compete with them.

From behind the goal line, the Evens were shouting instructions to their friends, shaking their arms to urge them on. Coach Brackett kept blowing his whistle as an added motivation. The whole arena became a noisy, crazy place, and Cody suddenly felt dizzy. He shook his head a few times to rid himself of the feeling, but it did no good. This was league hockey, all right, he thought. Tough and demanding.

Finally it was his heat's turn to line up on the goal line. The Odds sat down on the ice behind the Evens, attesting out loud to the difficulty of the "Manmaker" drill. Cody nervously took his position. He glanced to his left and then to his right. Next to him stood the red-haired boy who'd insulted Ernie on the outdoor rink the other day. The boy stared at him.

"Looks like you decided to join a real hockey team," he bragged to Cody.

Cody didn't know how to reply. He wasn't about to confess that he was on the ice without any official permission whatsoever. All he could muster was a "Yeah."

"Good for you," the boy said. "But just remember, only the best make it onto the Sharks."

Cody decided to ignore the boy. He didn't need any added pressure right now. He bent down low and poised his knees forward, his skates digging sharply into the ice. His body was an arrow waiting to be released by the starting signal.

"Go!"

Cody shoved off. He swung his arms and pumped his legs hard, keeping his eyes focused on the blue line in front of him. The players around him were a blur. He used every muscle in his body, gathering momentum. But the equipment he wore made him feel as if he were skating while giving his sister a piggyback ride. How are you supposed to get used to all this extra weight? he asked himself.

Cody was breathing heavily. The air in the arena seemed thinner and harder to take in than the fresh outdoor air he was used to breathing while skating. He wasn't sure how much more of this punishing drill he could take. His ankles were aching and his knees felt like wet noodles. But he drove on, striding down the ice as fast as he possibly could. He wanted to prove, to himself more than anyone else, that he belonged on the Transcona Sharks.

In time he passed a few skaters. His stride started loosening up, and his lungs seemed to catch a second wind. As the distances of each length increased, Cody found himself gaining more and more on the leading skaters. He started to feel as if he were back on the outdoor rink, skimming like a bird across the wide-open ice.

Soon he was among the top five. But, even without turning back to look, he knew the player behind him in sixth place was extremely close. Cody could hear his heavy breathing like a buzz in his ears.

Then the player suddenly moved in alongside him. It was the boy with the red hair. Cody knew he had to stay ahead somehow. That would show the boy he deserved a spot on the Sharks.

Only a little over one length of the ice surface was left in the drill. All that remained was to reach the goal line at the opposite end of the ice and return to the goal line where the drill had begun. Cody was panting with exhaustion, but he wasn't about to slow down. He could smell success.

As he approached the far goal line, Cody decided to try a quick stop and turn to give himself the split-second advantage he needed to beat the red-haired player. He dug his right toe into the ice hard and tried to pivot around in the opposite direction, all in one abrupt motion.

But he was moving too fast. During the pivot, Cody lost his balance, and before he knew it he toppled forward over his toe and onto the ice. He slid and crashed right into the boards behind the goal line like a sack of potatoes. The red-haired player sailed by, as did a whole flock of other players. Any hope of placing in the top five went crashing into the boards with him.

For an instant Cody considered just lying there and slinking off the ice into the showers. What's the use, anyhow? he thought. It's not like I'm actually going to be able to play with the team even if I make it.

"Get up! Get up!" he heard a voice calling to him. He turned and saw Ryan behind the boards, slapping his hand excitedly against the Plexiglas. "Come on, Cody, don't give up!"

He propelled himself up off the ice. He skated forward. He'd fallen behind, no doubt about it, but not so far that he still couldn't place ahead of the last few skaters. Cody pushed on. But his whole body hurt from the collision with the boards, and his new skates were starting to pinch his toes. His brain was sending messages to his legs, to push faster than they'd ever pushed before, but his legs just weren't listening. They needed a break. The ice surface might as well have been quicksand for all the speed Cody was able to muster. As he completed the drill, Cody looked back to see that there was nobody behind him. He had finished last.

What must the coach think of me? he thought. He lifted his eyes in the coach's direction, expecting the worst.

He couldn't believe his luck. Coach Brackett had probably not even noticed Cody coming in last place in the "Man-maker" drill. For some reason right now the coach's eyes were fastened on the boy who'd come in *second* last. Cody turned to take a closer look at the player. He'd taken off his helmet to get some air. It was Coach Brackett's son, Stu. And the coach didn't seem too pleased with him. He was muttering something under his breath.

That's odd, Cody reflected, you'd think the coach's son would be one of the best players on the team.

But that's not my problem, Cody reminded himself. Right now he had only one thing to consider: his one chance to play with the Transcona Sharks was not turning out at all as he had hoped.

5

Making a Mark

If any of you are too tired to continue," Coach Brackett suggested to the fifty boys gathered around him, "you're welcome to take a break now."

Some of the boys slackened their stances. But Cody, detecting a hint of sarcasm in the coach's voice, remained standing stiffly at attention.

The coach went on: "If you'd like, just stroll over to the dressing room, change into your street clothes, and walk out the front door of this arena." By now the sarcasm in his voice was more than a hint. "Because we don't need any quitters on the Transcona Sharks!" He emphasized each word by pounding his stick against the ice.

The players stood in silence.

"I plan on winning the City East championship this year," Coach Brackett went on. Droplets of moisture frosted his black moustache. "And I only want players on this team who share that plan. The B Team would be more than willing to accommodate any of you who want an easy ride. On this team, I take only serious hockey players: winners!"

The coach stepped forward, glaring at the boys, as if waiting for anyone who wanted to take him up on his offer to do so. Of course, nobody so much as stirred. It would be like admitting to everybody else that you were a quitter.

Cody shifted his weight from one skate to the other. He was anxious to get on with the practice. If only I could show Coach Brackett that I'm a winner, too, Cody thought.

"Let's move to some game situations," Coach Brackett said. "We can begin with a two-on-two drill."

Cody's heart skipped a beat. If there was one drill where he should be able to shine, this would be it. Two-on-two was all he ever played. He glanced up at the boys in the stands. They were still there, watching his every move, waiting for him to show his stuff.

The drill was simple. Two attackers were given the puck at centre ice and had to manoeuver past two defenders and shoot on net. There was no goaltender.

Cody's first turn came as a defender. Along with his partner, a tall boy who wore glasses underneath his helmet, Cody stood just in front of the blue line as Coach Brackett handed the puck to the two attackers, Travis and Kurt. Cody bounced on the heels of his skates, slightly crouched, and waited for the attackers to make their first move.

Travis took the puck and bolted down the right wing towards the tall player. Meanwhile, Kurt snuck far to Cody's right along the boards. Cody kept an eye on both players, slowly backtracking, keeping himself between the attackers and the net, his stick sweeping the ice. He was going to show Coach Brackett he was a smart player.

In the next moment Travis crossed the blue line and cut towards the net. Kurt did the same. At the same time the tall player decided to challenge Travis for the puck. He poked at the puck as Travis dribbled it down ice. But Travis managed to keep control of the black disk. He skated past the tall player and closer to the net.

Cody was all alone now.

He remained in position, his senses alert to everything around him. He was still between Travis and the net, but he'd had to leave Kurt open on his right. He decided his best bet was to force the play. He moved towards Travis, keeping his eyes on his opponent's shoulders, knowing that whatever move the attacker made would be signalled there.

Travis raised his head and scoped out his partner, then the net. Almost imperceptibly, his shoulders jerked in Kurt's direction.

Cody's body responded instantly. He stopped, as if on a dime, his forward movement towards Travis and fully extended his stick. Travis tried to hold back his pass, but he'd already made contact with the puck. The result was a weak putt that Cody had no trouble intercepting. He hooked the puck with the curve of his stick and reeled it in. Then, in one smooth motion, he cleared the puck past the centre line.

"Good job, young man," Coach Brackett hollered, patting Cody on the butt with his hockey stick. "That's the way to defend the two-on-two." He turned to the players lined up behind him. "I hope you guys were taking notes."

A feeling of relief and then of all-out elation washed over Cody's fatigued body. Now he was starting to get noticed. In the stands, the boys couldn't help themselves. They stood up and whistled enthusiastically.

Cody skated up ice and took his place in the attackers' line. Butterflies were spinning around inside his stomach, and he couldn't quite be sure whether they were from his excitement over the last play or his nervousness over how he would perform as an attacker.

"That was a great play, man," the tall boy he'd been paired with as a defender offered. "I sure would've looked bad if you hadn't made it."

"Thanks," Cody said. He kept his eyes on the action in front of him. He wanted to learn as much as possible from the mistakes other players made.

"My name's Deke Fenton," the boy added. "I haven't seen you at any of the other tryouts."

"I was at the first two," Cody lied, surprising himself with how easily and quickly the lie came. That's how badly he wanted to fit in. "Then I got sick and had to miss the last few. But I'm back now. My name's Cody Powell."

"This is my first year trying out for league hockey," Deke admitted.

"Mine, too," Cody volunteered.

So I'm not the only one on the ice today with no league experience, he thought. All of a sudden he felt a little less alone.

"Well, good luck," Deke said. "Hope you make the team."

Just the words "make the team" sent an odd thrill through Cody's body. "Hope you do, too," Cody told Deke. Now, more than ever, he wished he could join the Sharks. He belonged on this team.

Cody watched closely as the pair of attackers in front of him set up for their turn. He recognized only one of them, Stu Brackett. Stu took the puck and moved down ice, the other attacker far on the opposite wing. Then, all of a sudden, Stu and his partner crisscrossed. Cody had to admit that was a clever play. The defenders were confused, and Stu's partner managed to skate ahead towards the net. He was wide open. Then Stu stopped in his tracks, lined up the puck and whizzed it across the ice towards his partner. But way too far. Skating as fast as he could, the other attacker could not reach the puck, which hit the boards in the corner and ricocheted harmlessly onto a defender's stick. Stu wagged his head in frustration.

"Terrible, terrible, terrible," Coach Brackett roared, skating furiously towards Stu. "What kind of pass was that?"

Stu said nothing. He hung his head and shrugged his shoulders.

"I'll tell you what kind of pass that was." Coach Brackett's face was beet red. "That was the kind of pass that'll earn you a position on the B Team. I expect more from you, Stu, much more." He turned from his son and skated back to centre ice.

For a second Cody felt a chill run down his spine. Maybe it's not so easy being the coach's son, he thought. Suddenly he felt sorry for Stu.

Then it was Cody's turn. He was paired with a boy he recognized from school, Noah Rivard. Coach Brackett tossed the puck to Noah, who skated directly down centre ice towards the net. Cody looped to Noah's left, not too far off that a short pass couldn't reach him. The two defenders skated horizontally, closing the gap between them, forming a kind of wall about a metre behind the blue line.

Noah skated forward. Then, without looking, he snapped a pass to Cody. Cody needed but a single stride to reach the pass and took control of the puck. He took a few more strides and started to get the comfortable feeling on the ice he was used to on the outdoor rink. His legs felt free and strong. He gripped his stick tightly and pushed towards the defenders. Using Noah as a decoy, he careened past one defender, then faced the other.

Cody was in exactly the position he wanted. All the stickhandling practice he'd put in with his dad and with the boys had to pay off now. He shifted the puck from one side and then to the other, keeping his head up all the time. The defender skated backwards, keeping himself between Cody and the net. He knew what he was doing, Cody thought. Then he leaned down as if to send a wrist shot through the boy's legs. Expecting he'd have to block a shot, the boy hesitated a split second. In that brief time Cody slipped the puck to his left, and with his one-stride lead on the defender, skated toward the net, lifting an easy shot into the mesh of the goal.

Cody lifted his stick high in jubilation. From the stands he heard Mitch shouting, "Way to show 'em, Cody!"

Coach Brackett nodded his approval.

Cody was beginning to feel that given the chance he could make this team. No question about it.

The final drill of the practice Coach Brackett called "The Ultimate Face-Off." Two players stood together on the ice in the neutral zone as he shot the puck against the boards behind the goal. Whoever reached the puck first automatically became the attacker, the other player the defender. The attacker tried to score on the defender. As with the two-on-two drill, there was no goalie in the net.

For this drill Cody ended up matched against Stu Brackett. The two boys readied themselves for the drill, pressing their skates into the ice. Cody took a deep breath. He looked over at Stu and noticed that Stu's knees were shaking. He must really be nervous, Cody thought, even more nervous than I am. He couldn't understand why.

Bang! Coach Brackett's shot fired from his stick like a bullet, ricocheting against the boards and taking a hard bounce back towards the boys. They scrambled for possession of the black disk, kicking at it with the blades of their skates, poking at it with their sticks. Stu was trying hard, too hard, Cody thought. His movements were sloppy and abrupt. Cody focused his eyes on the puck and eventually managed to pry it loose. With his quick hands, he used his stick to direct the puck away from Stu. Stu tried to knock Cody off balance, but Cody refused to yield the puck.

Cody was still too far from the net to take a shot, so he tried skating away. But Stu was fast on his heels. He's really a hustler, Cody thought. I'll have to try something different. Then, suddenly, Cody stopped dead in his tracks. Having built up so much momentum, Stu went flying past him. Cody pushed forward and took a wrist shot. The puck tented the mesh of the net.

Howls of delight issued forth from his friends in the stands. This practice was turning out exactly as planned. Cody was proving that he could hold his own with league hockey players.

Cody retrieved the puck from the net, returned it to the coach, and skated back in line, Stu directly in front of him.

"That was close," Cody said. He didn't want Stu to feel too bad about losing in the drill. "I got lucky."

"You slashed me," Stu accused. "Otherwise, I would have had that puck."

"No I didn't."

"I'm sure my dad saw it," Stu said. "It was plain as day."

"I won that puck fair and square," Cody defended himself. He now regretted having felt sorry for Stu. Why's he being so ignorant? Cody thought.

"I'll show you next time we come up against each other," Stu said. His teeth were clenched. "I'll show my dad, too."

But there was no next time. After all the players had skated through the "Ultimate Face-Off" drill, Coach Brackett whistled the practice to an end. The fifty boys began loosening their equipment and filed off the ice. Most of them, Cody included, had only enough energy left to limp to the dressing room, if they could make it that far. Cody wondered if Coach Brackett had planned it that way.

As Cody stepped off the ice, Coach Brackett stopped him.

"Hold on there, young man," the coach said. He directed Cody to sit down on the bottom rung of the stands.

Uh-oh, Cody thought, here's where I get caught. Now what?

"What did you say your name was?" Coach Brackett asked Cody. In his hand he held a clipboard with a sheet of paper on it. Cody guessed that the names of all the players registered to play league hockey were printed on that sheet.

"Cody Powell," Cody replied. A sliver of fear shot through his stomach. Coach Brackett did not seem like the kind of guy you'd want to upset.

The coach lifted the sheet on the clipboard and tilted his head so that he could read down both its front and back sides. His eyebrows knitted together and his bottom lip jutted out.

"I can't find the name Cody Powell on my list," the coach continued, "and, come to think of it, I don't remember you from any other tryout. Did you just register this week?"

Cody considered lying, as he'd done earlier to Deke, but changed his mind quickly. What use would lying be anyhow? "No, I didn't just register," he told the coach.

"What do you mean?" the coach asked, obviously baffled.

Cody looked Coach Brackett in the eye. "Well, the truth is I don't have the money to register. I just came out today because I wanted to see what it would be like. To play league hockey, I mean."

The corners of the coach's mouth creased. Cody figured Coach Brackett was smiling, but he couldn't be sure.

"Is that right?" the coach asked. "You want to play hockey for us so badly that you just snuck into our practice?"

"Yes, sir," Cody replied.

A curious snicker emerged from the coach's lips. "That's wonderful, absolutely wonderful. We need players with your kind of dedication and initiative on this team. Not to mention your kind of stickhandling abilities. You have a great touch with the puck, Cody. I bet you could score a whole lot of goals in this league."

Cody felt as if he'd just been expressed twenty flights up an elevator. He couldn't believe what the coach was telling him. It was too good to be true.

"Although you could sure use some new equipment," Coach Brackett added. "That stuff you're wearing looks two sizes too big for you. And those gloves! Did your grandpa loan them to you?"

Cody grinned, but just to be polite. Those beat-up old gloves were his favourite piece of equipment. They were his dad's once, and last year he'd presented them to Cody.

Just then Stu emerged from the dressing room. He was carrying his duffel bag over his shoulder, the stick popping out one side. He gave Cody a cold once-over.

"Dad, I picked up all the late registration forms from the guys and put away the pucks," Stu said eagerly. "Is there anything else I can do?"

Coach Brackett absently dug through his jacket pockets and pulled out a set of keys. The keyholder was a miniature hockey puck. "No, Stu, that's it," he said, handing the keys to his son. "Just put your stuff away in the trunk. I'll meet you and your mom outside in a few minutes."

Stu readjusted the duffel bag on his shoulder, his eyes dropping to the floor.

"OK, Dad."

Coach Brackett moved closer to Cody. "You remind me a lot of myself when I was your age," he confided. "Of course, you're not nearly physical enough out on the ice, but you've got great moves, on offence and defence, and you use your brains. I was like that, too, you know, always thinking out on the ice."

"Thanks," Cody said. "That's why I came here today. To find out if I had what it takes to make the Sharks." He smiled. "Now I know."

Stu had already turned to leave but out of the corner of his eye Cody caught him hanging back within earshot.

"You say you just can't come up with the registration money, huh?" Coach Brackett asked.

"That's right. I live with my mom, and she can't afford to let me play league hockey. This equipment, except for the skates, the stick, and my gloves, are my buddy's." Cody pointed to Ryan up in the stands. "If I registered, it would cost my mom more than she's willing to pay."

The coach chewed the cap of his pen. "The club does have a program for kids like you," he said. "We can make arrangements to pay most of the costs, if your mom'll just sign a few forms and pay the difference."

Cody couldn't believe his ears. "I'm sure she will," he said. "She knows how much playing league hockey means to me."

Coach Brackett patted Cody on the shoulder. "Son, we could really use someone with your stickhandling abilities on the left wing."

At that moment Cody noticed Stu stomping rapidly towards the arena exit, his footsteps echoing loudly through the empty arena. He slammed the door behind him. Cody figured he must really be upset about his performance that afternoon.

Coach Brackett apparently hadn't heard a thing. He was riffling through a pile of papers at his side. He handed Cody two sheets.

"Have we got ourselves a deal?" he asked. "You get your mom to sign these forms, and I'll hold a spot for you on this team until our first game, next Tuesday."

Cody was on top of the world. He took the coach's hand and shook it vigorously. Coach Brackett might be tough, he thought, but he's a winner. I like that.

"You've got yourself a deal," he exclaimed.

6

Divorced with Children

"Cody! Tish!" Cody's mom called from the kitchen. "The phone's for you."

The family had just come back from church, where they went every Sunday morning at Tish's insistence, ever since the divorce. When the phone rang, Cody had been modelling his new Transcona Sharks uniform for Tish in the living room. His little sister was chasing him around the coffee table, begging him to let her try on the uniform, too.

"Just for a second," she had cried.

"No, it's all mine," Cody had teased.

Two days ago Cody had taken the forms, signed by his mother, back to Coach Brackett, along with two hundred dollars, most of which came from exchanging his new skates. Now, as the turquoise and grey uniform with the Sharks insignia on the front proved, he was an official member of the Transcona Sharks: Number 18, Cody Powell.

"Hurry up, kids!" his mom shouted again.

Cody ran to the kitchen, Tish tagging close behind him, both of them giggling uncontrollably. She had one hand on the new jersey and was trying to force it off his shoulders.

"It's long distance!"

Long distance? Cody thought. That could mean Uncle Tim and Aunt Sheila in Toronto. Or Grandma in Hamilton. Or ...

Or his dad in Kamloops. His face sunk. He was still in no mood to speak with his dad.

"It's your dad," his mom confirmed, as Cody and Tish took a seat in the kitchen. "He'd like to talk to you. Both of you," she emphasized, handing Cody the phone.

"I have nothing to say," Cody grumbled, pushing the phone into Tish's hands. "You talk."

Tish took hold of the phone readily. "Hi, Dad!" she exclaimed. "How are you?"

Cody remained seated at the kitchen table, his hands crossed at the chest, his face sulky. His mom stood next to him. She rubbed his shoulder with her hand.

"We're all fine," Tish said happily. Her whole body was alive with excitement. "I got an A on my spelling test, Cody made the hockey team, and Mom's quit smoking."

Cody's mom squirmed. "Stick to the important news," she muttered.

"I wrote you a letter, Dad. I hope you get it before Christmas, so you know what to get me. How will you send me my gift? Does Santa Claus pass through Kamloops on his way here from the North Pole?"

Cody stuck out his tongue and rolled his eyes, making a "gag me!" face. His mom shot him a scolding glance.

In the next second, Tish let out a piercing shriek of glee.

"Really, Dad? I'd love that." She closed her eyes tight as if to better let the good news sink in. "And you already talked about it with Mom, and she said it was OK?"

Cody's head turned in bewilderment from Tish to his mom. He searched his mom's face with pleading eyes for an explanation.

"Your father will tell you," she whispered to him.

Suddenly, Tish caught on to Cody's discomfort. She looked at him with genuine concern in her eyes.

"But, Dad, Cody has to want to, too," she said into the phone.

"Want what?" Cody asked out loud. "What's going on here?"

Again he was overcome with a feeling of powerlessness. Ever since his mom and dad's divorce, he had been feeling more and more left out. Like he wasn't important anymore.

"I think you'd better talk to him yourself, Dad," Tish said. She cautiously handed the phone to Cody. "Dad wants to ask you something," she said. Her green eyes softened. "Just give him a chance."

Cody was curious, all right, to find out what his dad wanted to ask him. But that's not why he decided to take the phone from Tish and talk to him. He would do it, he told himself, only because his little sister had asked him to.

"Yeah?" Cody mumbled into the phone.

"How are you, Cody?" his dad asked. "I've missed you." His voice seemed hesitant, almost nervous.

"Fine, I guess." Cody wasn't about to say much. But something inside him made him say just enough to keep the conversation going. He had to admit that it felt good to hear his father's voice again.

"Tish tells me you made the hockey team."

"Yeah."

"That's fantastic!"

"I haven't played in a game yet."

"Well, I'm sure you'll do well."

"I'll do my best."

"I wish" — Cody detected a crack in his dad's voice — "I could help you practise. Like we used to in the rink I built in the back yard."

If that's what his dad wished, Cody thought, why wasn't he doing it? Why was he still in Kamloops?

Cody felt a lump in his throat and his nose sniffled, but he fought back the urge to cry.

"Whatever," he mumbled.

"Maybe we can practise again," his dad said. He seemed to be hurrying his words, trying to get them all out as fast as possible. "That's why I called you."

Cody didn't know what to make of his dad's last statement. What did he mean? Was there a chance he was coming back to Winnipeg again? He didn't want to get his hopes up too high.

"I've discussed this with your mother," his dad continued. "We've arranged for you and Tish to take the train out here on Boxing Day and stay until a week or so after New Year's. You can both use your mother's CN pass, so getting here won't cost a thing, and you'll still be able to spend Christmas Day with your mother." Cody heard a baby wail in the background and the shuffling sounds of someone rushing to calm it. "Della and I would love to have you."

Cody sat silently, a hundred different feelings swirling around inside him. His stomach felt suddenly upset. His head hurt. His eyes burned. What was he supposed to say?

On the phone there was only the electric silence of the long distance connection.

"Tish has already agreed," his dad said. "We're just waiting for your decision."

Cody tried to collect his thoughts, but there was no way he could. For some reason he remembered a dream he'd once had where he was trying to run home and the streets kept changing on him, confusing him. He felt the same way now. He'd like to see his dad again — that would mean a lot to him. But not out in Kamloops, with a whole new family. And, besides, he had the Transcona Sharks to think of. In the two weeks or so he'd be away in Kamloops, they'd probably play three or four games. How could he miss them? Then again, there was a whole season of games ahead, but when would he have a chance to see his dad again?

"What do you say, son?" his dad persisted.

Cody cradled the phone between his neck and shoulder and held his head in his hands. Then he looked at Tish. Still in her Sunday clothing, a white blouse with a billowy skirt, she looked like one of those little girls from *Little House on the Prairie*. She was holding out her hands in a begging attitude, mouthing the word "please!" over and over again.

Cody wanted to make Tish happy. He really did. But this was so complicated. Everything was so complicated ever since the divorce.

"Cody?" his dad's voice reached out to him over the phone.

Cody pulled the phone back to his mouth.

His dad had taken a lot of things away from him, Cody thought, since he'd left their family. Cody couldn't let him take away the Transcona Sharks, too.

"No," he said. And then he handed the phone to his mom.

7

Cody Alone

The sun was a blazing disk of yellow in the grey sky. Cody squinted in its bright rays as he stepped out into the backyard, and the door slammed behind him. Right now he needed to be alone.

He considered tramping over to "the Igloo" to meet one of the guys or to just do some thinking, but beneath the parka he'd thrown on as he left the house, he was still wearing his dress shirt and pants from church. In his hand he tightly held the Transcona Sharks jersey.

He kicked at the shovel that lay in the middle of the sidewalk — he'd left it there himself last time he'd shovelled — and sat down on one of the cold plastic seats of the teeter-totter. A biting wind pierced his cheeks. He didn't care. The cold suited perfectly the lousy way he was feeling right now.

In front of him, buried under a good three feet of snow between the garage and the neighbour's fence, was the spot where, ever since he was three years old, his dad had built a little rink for the two of them to skate on.

Each fall his dad would box in the area where the rink would be with a series of two-by-fours and keep the area clear of snow. Then, when the temperature dropped below zero for over a week, he would flood the area with water from the garden hose. Usually, he'd have to flood the rink about three or four times, until the ice was good and thick. Then the rink would be ready to skate on, and Cody and his father, and sometimes his mom and Tish, would put on their skates in the house and walk outside to play hockey. Cody had learned to skate on that rink, using a chair from the kitchen for support, and how to shoot the puck, too. Of course, in the summer the grass in that part of the back yard was paler than the rest, and Cody's mom often complained that his dad was ruining the lawn, but Cody always saw the yellowed area as a reminder of the fun that the winter ahead promised. In fact, the rink used to make him proud of his dad. He didn't know of any other dads who built rinks in their back yards.

Cody's eyes now searched the mounds of snow in the back yard for some trace of the rink. There was none. The rink had disappeared. Just like his dad.

Almost against his will, Cody started thinking again about his mom and dad's divorce. As hard as he tried, he never really could understand it. He could follow Tish's example, he thought, and act like the divorce never happened, but that seemed impossible for him. The divorce was there, like it or not. There were times when he wished there were someone he could ask for answers, someone who could explain what had been going on — maybe a teacher, or one of his friends whose parents were also divorced — but he always decided that no one could help him. He had to make sense of this all by himself.

Cody didn't know when it had all started, when his mom and his dad had started pulling apart. He did remember, though, how much they'd argued, most of the time over things Cody couldn't quite understand. Some nights after they had been screaming at each other, Cody's mom would finally say, "Stop it, Doug, we'll wake the kids." Cody always used to think that showed how stupid adults could be. Didn't they know they'd already woke him and his sister? Sometimes, at that point, Cody's dad would walk out the back door and drive off in the car. Those were the times that made Cody and Tish most afraid. He'd have to read Tish's favourite book until she'd fallen asleep again. After a while Cody had memorized the book — *Pepito's Story* — so well that he didn't even have to turn on his hockey player night light to read it.

Outside now in the winter cold Cody started to cry. The tears streamed down his face. He lifted his Transcona Sharks jersey to his cheeks and used it to wipe away the wetness.

The fights had grown worse over the months, until the summer before last, when his dad had finally moved out. He still came by, though, to see Cody and Tish almost every evening, and every day after school Cody would wait for him outside the particle board plant where he worked. On those days his dad would let Cody ride double with him on his bicycle, and he'd drop Cody off at home. Things hadn't seemed that bad yet.

Then Cody's dad had met Della. Soon he started visiting the house less and less often, and when he did the shouting matches with Cody's mom became more and more vicious. His dad became awkward around Cody and Tish, as if he knew that what he was doing to them was wrong and didn't want to face it. By the time fall had arrived, he hardly ever called the house.

And he didn't come by to build the outdoor rink.

Then one day a few months ago, Cody's dad announced he was leaving for Kamloops with Della and her two kids. That was about the time Cody had decided he wasn't speaking to him anymore. Cody still wasn't convinced he hadn't made the right decision.

The freezing wind prickled Cody's face. He realized suddenly that he was shivering and his teeth were actually chattering from the cold. He stood up and pulled on his Transcona Sharks jersey. It felt great. He ran his hands over the round crest on the chest. He couldn't wait to play that Tuesday in his first game with the Sharks. Before then he'd go down to the Hockey Hut Swap Shop and have the owner press the name POWELL across the back.

Cody turned back towards the house. He spotted his sister looking down at him from behind the frosted bedroom window. She waved at him. He smiled back. She'll understand, Cody thought, whatever I choose to do.

There was no way he'd give up playing on the Sharks to visit his dad. But he'd insist that Tish make the trip. She really wanted to, he could see that, and he wouldn't want to do anything to make her sad.

As he stepped back inside the house, Cody wasn't crying anymore.

8

On the Sharks

O ver here! I'm open!"
Cody lifted his eyes from the puck in front of him and searched for the source of the voice. It wasn't easy, he conceded, seeing through the bars of a face guard. Finally, he sighted Noah waving at him across the width of the neutral zone. In his rush to deliver the pass, Cody ended up connecting with the shank of the stick rather than the blade. The puck rolled over the ice, wobbly and weak, reaching Noah at a standstill.

"You have to get more wood on it, kid," an onlooker yelled from somewhere in the stands.

Mind your own business, Cody couldn't help thinking.

The Sharks Line Two forwards now moved into the attack. Noah, tall and strong, on the right wing. The red-haired boy — by now Cody had learned his name was Derrick — lanky and sharp-shooting at centre. And Cody, a nervous wreck on skates, on the left wing.

This was the first of two exhibition games for the Transcona Sharks before the regular season began in exactly one week. But, as Cody kept reminding himself, for him this wasn't just the first game of the season. This was his very first ice time in his very first league game — ever.

"Go! Go! Go!" Coach Brackett shouted from the visitors' bench. "Create your own opportunities!"

The Sharks were playing against the Elmwood Elks, a scrappy, physical club prone to penalties when they were behind. In the dressing room before the game, the coach had preached on the importance of taking an early lead. He wanted a goal, and fast.

With a burst of sudden speed, Noah split the neutral zone. At centre ice he tossed a pass to Derrick. Derrick ploughed over his man, carefully dribbling the puck in front of him, then flew to his left.

All of a sudden the Sharks were on a three-on-two drive.

"Press the net!" Coach Brackett urged. His face was purple with excitement. "Press the net!"

Cody tried to keep pace, but he felt lost. Under the bright, glaring lights of the Elks Arena, everything on the ice seemed to blur. The cheers and boos from the fans echoed inside the four corrugated steel walls like funhouse shrieks of laughter. In fact, if Cody didn't know any better, he'd swear the ice surface itself was shifting and shaking beneath his skates just like the floor of a funhouse. His topsy-turvy stomach would attest to that. He half wished the action would steer away from him, at least for now.

The three Sharks skated into the Elks zone, Derrick still controlling the puck, Noah wide to the right, Cody doing his best to keep up on the left side. The Elks defenders fanned out to protect their goal. Their goalie crouched at the ready, his bulky equipment blocking the net.

Just outside the Elks blue line, Derrick coasted a moment, his head held up high and turning quickly to the right and left. He was obviously considering how best to penetrate the opposing zone.

Cody pumped his legs hard. "Press the net!" the coach had commanded, so now he pushed forward. He would do his part on this play, he decided, not just hang around on the outskirts, trying to keep out of the way.

"Wait!" Derrick shouted.

But it was too late. Cody's skates had already crossed the blue line. As Noah lunged forward to catch Derrick's leading pass, which would have given him an easy breakaway on the Elks goalie, the referee blew his whistle.

"Offside!" he declared, indicating the infraction with a raised hand.

As the players moved back into the neutral zone for the face-off, Derrick charged towards Cody, his face livid with rage.

"You're supposed to wait for the puck to cross the blue line before you do. Otherwise you're offside. Didn't anyone teach you that?"

"Study the rule book, kid!" a parent taunted from the stands.

Cody closed his eyes and rattled his head. He knew all about offsides, but he'd never played with them. When he played on the outdoor rink with the guys, there was no such thing as an offside. You just skated around the ice wherever you wanted to.

Derrick turned to Noah. "I knew that Cody kid wasn't ready for league hockey," he grumbled.

"It was just an offside," Noah answered back. "It could have happened to anyone. Let's give him a chance. He did just fine in practice."

Derrick spat onto the ice. "Practice is one thing, but this is a game," he muttered under his breath. "A league game. Not shinny."

Trying to ignore Derrick's tirade, Cody looked up at the stands surrounding the ice. But there wasn't a single familiar face. Ryan, Mitch, and Ernie had no way of getting to the arena. And his mom had to attend her monthly meeting at union head-quarters. Tish was staying with the woman across the street.

As for Deke, the only boy who'd been friendly to Cody during the tryout practice, even he was not around today. He'd been cut from the Sharks and had to settle for playing on the B Team. Cody wondered how he'd taken the news.

Cody was all alone. But maybe it was best that way. Because he couldn't say for sure how well he was going to perform.

The referee dropped the puck at that moment and the action resumed. Cody promised himself to keep his head up and play carefully. No more stupid mistakes.

Derrick won the face-off and sent the puck flying to Noah. Noah couched it with the blade of his stick and cut towards the net, crossing the blue line. Then an Elks defenceman rocketed towards the right winger, and Noah tossed the puck over to Cody, who was now only a few metres away from the opposing goal. Here was Cody's chance to make something happen.

The defenceman covering Cody smartly forced him wide to the left of the net. Cody took stock of the boards next to him and then lurched to his right, trying to beat the defender. But the defender stuck to him, so Cody retreated. He swirled back just inside the blue line and looked to make a pass. But Derrick and Noah were covered. Cody decided to make one more rush for the net.

He moved ahead. So did the defender. Then, instantly, the defender was upon him, trying to strip Cody of the puck. Cody kicked the puck to his left, then nudged it forward with his stick. Next he deked left and slipped the puck under the defender's stick. Suddenly he had room to make a play.

A surge of adrenalin shot through Cody's body. From the stands he heard a roaring cheer. This was real hockey! he thought.

Then, just like in the outdoor games Cody was used to playing, a kind of sixth sense told him exactly where the goal was. He reared in that direction. In front of him, though, were two Elks forwards, who'd fallen back to support their defencemen.

Out of the corner of his eye, Cody spotted Noah open next to the net. He made the pass. The puck connected with Noah's stick. Wasting no time, Noah one-timed the puck at the goalie. It was going in. But at the last second the Elks goalie kicked out his pad and blocked the puck. The puck bounced behind the net.

"Grab the rebound!"

Emboldened now, Cody heaved towards the loose puck. So did the two Elks defencemen. In no time there was a mad scramble against the boards of skates, sticks, elbows, and knees. From the Sharks bench, Cody could hear Coach Brackett yell, "Get that puck! Make the play!"

But Cody was being knocked about like a pinball by the Elks defenders. He had no idea how to protect himself. He waited for the referee to call a penalty, but no whistle came. All the jostling was more or less the result of each of the players trying to get to the puck.

Finally, the puck was pried loose. In the same instant, Cody found himself sprawled on the ice. He had let himself be decked. An Elks defenceman picked up the free puck and cleared it to one of his forwards. Then he turned to Cody. "Where'd you get those gloves?" he snickered. "At the museum?"

Shocked, Cody remained on the ice a few seconds, trying to comprehend what had just occurred.

"Get up off your butt!" Derrick snarled. "Time to play defence."

"Wake up!" a parent shouted.

Cody picked himself up and hustled back to the Sharks end of the ice. But too late. As far back from the action as he was right now, the Elks might as well have been on a power play. Cody watched, feeling more like an observer than a participant, as the Elks forwards took advantage of the fast break. The right winger passed to the centre. He backhanded a pass to the left winger, who in turn slapped a hard shot at the Sharks net. If not for a last-second glove save from the Sharks goalie, Eddie Bruska, the Elks would have had a one-goal lead. All because of Cody's blunder up ice.

Cody skated back and tapped Eddie on the hip.

"Thanks for saving my butt," he told the goalkeeper.

Eddie nodded. Then from the bench Coach Brackett hollered, "Line change." Cody's first shift as a member of the Transcona Sharks was over. He thanked his lucky stars that the game was still a scoreless tie and skated to the bench.

Frustrated over having been bullied out of the play deep in the other team's end, Cody slumped down onto the bench, as Line One took the ice. Coach Brackett approached him. His face was drawn into hard lines.

"You're out there to score goals. You can't do that sitting on your rear end."

"I'm sorry," Cody said, shaking his head.

"Don't be afraid to mix it up with the other guys," the coach admonished. Cody couldn't tell whether he was angry or just handing out advice. "You have to learn to protect yourself. There's a lot of physical play in our games."

"I can see that," Cody admitted.

"The important thing is to set your legs hard," the coach went on, "so you always keep your balance. Don't worry so much about the puck. If you're the last one standing, you'll find the puck. Or it'll find you. Believe me."

"OK, Coach."

"And another thing," Coach Brackett added, "that stick-handling of yours ..."

Cody's heart sank. What was the coach going to complain about now?

"... it's great. You're just what we need to help this team make it to the city finals."

Cody breathed a deep sigh of relief. "I hope so," he answered. He was glad Coach Brackett seemed to be on his side. He's not such a mean guy, Cody thought.

Cody squirted a water bottle over his sweating face and sat back to watch the Sharks Line One players. He knew he still had a lot to learn about league hockey. Shutting out the noises and glare in the arena around him, Cody concentrated on the action on the ice.

The first thing he noticed was that Coach Brackett's son, Stu, like himself, played left wing. Maybe that's why he hasn't been so friendly to me, Cody concluded, because he's worried that I'll steal his spot as the Line One left winger. But no matter how he talked, Coach Brackett would never do that, Cody thought, not to his own son. I know my dad never would. Cody caught himself. As far as he was concerned, he reminded himself, his dad had done a lot worse.

Cody brought his mind back to hockey. Presently the Sharks had dumped the puck deep into the Elks end and their three forwards were chasing it down. Travis, the Line One centre and the captain of the team, reached the puck first and fed it to Kurt, who was planted at the point. Kurt lifted his stick over his head and brought it down in a tight arc. Bang! His slapshot ricocheted off the crossbar.

"Score the goal! Score the goal!"

The players on the Sharks bench, Cody included, were on their feet, urging their teammates on. Coach Brackett was so involved in the action that his whole body from the knees up was leaning across the boards and over the ice.

"Come on, guys, press!" The coach leaned even further out. "Stu, get in there, mix it up, get your stick on the puck."

As if hearing his dad, Stu lunged at the rebound. He snagged it with his stick and skated to his right, looking for an open spot from which to shoot. Meanwhile, Travis headed to the net and hovered just in front of the goalie.

"Pass it, Stu," Coach Brackett yelled. "Trav's in the open."

But Stu must have spotted a hole in the Elks defensive blockade. He snapped his wrists and sent a shot straight at the net. It was a floater, waist high and slow. Travis tried to deflect the puck but it was too far to reach. The goalie gloved the puck handily.

The referee whistled for a face-off.

"Line Three, get in there," Coach Brackett commanded.

The Line One players skated to the bench.

"Did you see me nab that rebound?" Stu asked his dad excitedly as he took his place on the bench, only two players down from Cody. "There must have been three Elks around me."

"Yes, I saw it," Coach Brackett answered, "but why didn't you pass the puck to Travis? He would have had an easy shot on net."

Stu's face paled. He puffed out a deep breath. "I thought I could score," he said.

"That's fine," Coach Brackett said. He patted his son on the shoulder. "But you've got to try to play smarter. Keep your eyes wide open to everything around you."

"I'm trying, Dad," Stu appealed. "I really am."

"I know that. But I'm sure you can do better."

Cody had listened closely to the conversation. Maybe the coach had come down hard on Stu, but everything he had told him made perfect sense. He repeated Coach Brackett's words silently to himself, vowing to follow the coach's advice. If you wanted to play winning hockey, Cody realized, you had to play smart and keep your eyes wide open. And you had to play physical, as the coach had pointed out to Cody earlier. Stu was lucky, Cody decided, to have a dad who knew so much about hockey. He couldn't wait for his next shift. He knew now exactly what he had to do.

9

He Shoots, He Scores

O ver here!" Travis called out.

Stu swept past the Elks defender and spotted his centre open to the left of the net. This time he bore down and made the pass. The puck travelled through a gaggle of players and found Travis's stick. Travis sliced at it. The puck rose off the ice and veered to the net. The Elks goalie shot out his blocking pad. But too late. The puck swished past the goalie's arm and into the net.

The Sharks raised their sticks in celebration. All the players on the ice hurried to congratulate Stu and Travis.

On the bench, Coach Brackett jumped for joy. "Nice pass, Stu!" he cried. "We needed that one."

With only three minutes remaining in the game, the score was now tied at one, the Elks having scored a power-play goal early in the second period. This first game of the season for both teams was proving to be a close one.

Coach Brackett called the Line One players to the bench. They were flying high, describing the goal to one another over and over again. Stu's face was filled with a wide grin.

"Good work, boys," the coach said. "Take a rest now and we'll put you back in for the final minute. Line Two, get out there, and see what you can do."

Cody leapt over the boards and onto the ice, feeling pumped and ready. He felt his play had improved consider-

ably over the last two periods. He'd been able to stand his
ground with the stronger Elks players and managed to avoid
getting caught offside again. He'd forechecked and back-
checked, and in the last minute of the second period he'd
created a breakaway when he threaded a perfect pass across
the centre line to Noah.

Even the noisy buzz inside the arena was no longer so
much a nuisance to Cody as it was a beat that urged him on.

Now, he wheeled around the face-off circle waiting for the
referee to signal the resumption of the action. Finally, the
referee stepped into the centre ice circle. Cody stopped and
tensed for the face-off.

The puck dropped. Cody kept his eyes glued to it, as
Derrick and the Elks centre battled for possession. Eventually
the Elks centre outmuscled Derrick. The puck went flying
into the Sharks zone.

As the Elks forwards passed the puck between them,
Cody speeded back to help with the defence. Along with the
two other Sharks forwards, Cody positioned himself behind
the puck, creating a wall of turquoise and grey jerseys.

The Elks forwards continued their precision passing, trying to open up a hole in the Sharks defence. Finally, Derrick
grew impatient and fell for the bait. As the right winger he
was covering stickhandled the puck, Derrick attacked him.
The winger quickly sent a pass to his centre and skated forward for the give-and-go. Derrick was left at least three paces
behind the play, as his man picked up the return pass and
charged the net, the puck cradled in the blade of his stick.

Cody decided to pick up the loose winger. He skated
across the ice, his stick flung out in front of him to block any
sudden shot.

The winger then twisted his stick far behind his back and
set up for the slapshot. Cody decided that he was close
enough to block the shot with his body. I might as well put

Ryan's equipment to good use, he thought, as he clamped his eyes shut and threw his body onto the ice in front of the Elks sniper to form a human shield.

The shot never came. As Cody reopened his eyes, he saw Derrick hook his stick between the Elks player's skates and lift him off his feet. The winger went tumbling to the ice, while Derrick picked up the loose puck. Instantly, the referee blasted his whistle.

"Tripping!" he called. "Two minutes."

As the referee turned his back to skate to the scorekeeper, Derrick cursed under his breath and slowly made his way to the penalty box.

Now the Sharks were really in trouble, having to play short-handed. Cody had never before had to kill a penalty. He thought of his responsibilities. Protect the net. Clear the puck as far as possible — no icing could be called on the defending team during a penalty. And when you control the puck, waste as much time as possible. More than ever, he'd have to play smart hockey.

The Elks took the face-off and moved into their power-play positioning. This time the Elks forwards edged towards the Sharks net, while their defencemen stood back and played the point. Cody's job was to cover the defencemen. He followed the path of the puck as they passed to each other, feeling a lot like the monkey in the middle in a schoolyard game of Keep-Away.

Cody waited patiently. Something had to give.

The mistake came as one of the Elks defencemen tried to sneak a pass past Cody to the forward situated directly in front of the Sharks goal crease. The defenceman miscalculated by a few centimetres. That was all the slack Cody needed. He reached out and knocked the puck free. Noah skated up and gathered the puck in, then flicked it over the blue line and into the neutral zone. That gave the Sharks enough time to regroup.

As during the practice, Cody felt encumbered by his heavy equipment as he chased down Noah's clearing shot. He wished he could tear it all off and skate down the ice dressed only in a shirt and pants. Then Cody chuckled to himself. He thought of the whole hour Ryan had spent yesterday afternoon teaching him how to properly put on all the different pieces. The cup, the pants, the socks, the shin pads, the elbow pads. Cody had been reminded of the times his mom had tried to teach him how to tie a necktie. He'd been about as clumsy, too, at putting on the equipment as he'd been with the tie.

Now, ignoring as best he could his bulky gear, he moved up the ice to harass the Elks player with the puck. He tried to concentrate on preventing the opposing attackers from moving the puck back into the Sharks zone. But then the player with the puck suddenly overskated it. In a flash, Cody pounced on the free puck. He kicked it forward onto his stick and raced past the centre line.

Cody looked ahead of him. Even though his was the team playing short-handed, Cody appreciated the fact that there was one less player out on the ice. That gave him more room to manoeuvre and put his stickhandling to use. Like a spinning top he now zigzagged over the ice, keeping the puck in his possession. His intention was to kill as much time as possible, but to his right he saw Noah flying forward and realized that his teammate was intent on spearheading an offensive drive into the Elks zone.

Cody pushed the puck forward to Noah, who swept it up without losing so much as a single stride. Meanwhile, the Elks, pressing on the power play, had been caught with only two players back. With just over a minute remaining on the clock, Cody found himself in a two-on-two situation, without question his strong suit.

Noah angled towards the net, Cody doing the same from the opposite direction. As the two forwards crossed paths, Noah left the puck for Cody, while breaking for the net. Noah's clever playmaking had fooled one of the Elks defenders. Only one defender now stood in front of the Elks goalie.

Cody edged closer. Then, carefully, he aimed a pass at Noah, who was now crossing the blue line. Noah took the pass and lined up for the shot. He brought his stick down hard against the puck, which went whizzing over the defender's stick. The goalie dove to his left to stop the shot. His raised goalie pad just barely deflected the puck. Cody picked up the rebound and chopped it high into the net.

A goal!

Cody threw his stick into the air and let out a wild shriek of joy, letting out all the pressure that had built up inside him. The whole arena must have been able to hear him.

The scoreboard read: HOME 1, VISITORS 2. On the clock: 00:58. Cody's Line Two teammates rushed to embrace him. He felt now as if he really belonged on the Transcona Sharks. He had earned the respect of his teammates.

"Way to play heads-up hockey, Cody," Coach Brackett enthused as Cody skated to the bench. "I knew you could do it."

"You just graduated to the big leagues, kid," Derrick shouted from the penalty box.

Cody drank in the cheers and congratulations. Then, for an instant, he found himself wishing his dad were around to see his first-ever league hockey goal.

As it turned out, that goal won the game for the Sharks.

Cody was the hero of the day.

10

Dressing Room Clash

The scene inside the dressing room reminded Cody of a party. But this party was different. Even though there were some parents around, including Coach Brackett, none of them seemed to care what the kids did. They could be as loud and wild as they wanted.

As soon as the boys had entered the dressing room, Derrick switched on a CD player that blasted rap music. Now a bunch of guys stood on the changing bench in half dress shaking their butts and swigging pop. Travis was carrying Eddie, the goalie, around the room on his shoulders, taking him to all the players so they could rub his head. Noah was displaying his slapshot ... in the showers! And a photographer from the *Transcona Views* was snapping pictures for the upcoming newspaper.

This is fun! Cody thought, taking the chaos in.

He sat on the bench, carefully removing Ryan's equipment. Every so often one of his fellow Sharks would approach him and congratulate him on scoring the game-winning goal. Cody beamed. Then, before he put away his jersey in his duffel bag, he touched once again the crest on the front and the number 18 on the back. He looked at the name POWELL printed across the shoulders and swelled with pride. He couldn't wait to tell his mom and Tish about today's game.

"Boys, can I just have your attention for a moment, please?" Coach Brackett cut in then. The players hooted and hollered.

The coach grinned. Then he pushed out his hands, asking for quiet. The decibel level in the room dropped a few notches.

"I just want to say a few things," he went on. "First of all, you played excellent hockey tonight." He looked around the room, his eyes acknowledging every player. "Each and every one of you."

The players sent a whoop reverberating through the room.

"If we play this kind of hockey all season long, I have no question in my mind that we'll make the city finals." He licked his lips. "I think we just might win the finals, too."

"Champs! Champs! Champs!" the boys chanted.

Again the coach held out his hands. Behind his black moustache, he was smiling widely.

"Now, about the next game. It's our last exhibition game, but it's an important one all the same." His eyes fired up. "We're playing the St. Vital Marauders, and I'm sure all of you who played league hockey last year can remember them."

Several players booed and hissed.

The coach nodded his head. "Somehow," he said, "this year I have a feeling the Marauders are not going to keep us out of the city finals." In the next instant, he took a few steps in Cody's direction. Cody had no idea what was going on.

"I'm really pleased," the coach continued, "with the play of the new members of this team." He leaned down and pulled Cody off the bench, draping his right arm around Cody's shoulders. "I think this particular new player right here just might be exactly what we need to beat the Marauders."

He shook Cody's hand. "Good job, son," he said.

Several players applauded.

Then, from across the dressing room, Travis called out, "Let's give Cody a nickname, Coach. To make him an official member of this team."

"Yeah," Noah added from his spot on the bench. "Cody's just too boring."

"He's a stickhandling wizard, that's for sure," Travis commented. "How about Wiz?"

"Wiz!" the other boys in the dressing room repeated loudly.

Coach Brackett held Cody's right hand high up into the air. "Wiz it is," he proclaimed.

Cody slinked back onto the bench. Suddenly, he felt embarrassed. He wasn't used to being fussed over. In the mirror running the length of the bench he noticed that he had begun blushing.

"That's all I have to say," the coach concluded. "Except that I'm glad you're enjoying your victory, boys, but there's another team slated to use this room in fifteen minutes, so get a move on it." He laughed. "Anyone who wants to can meet at Dal's Restaurant in half an hour for pizza. It's on me!"

The boys cheered once again.

In a while the dressing room began emptying, as parents came to the door, keys in hand, to pick up their kids. Cody decided to take his time. Coach Brackett had promised him a ride home, and the coach would probably be one of the last to leave the arena. Eyes closed, he sat back now, his bare shoulders against the cool cement wall of the dressing room, savouring his first game with the Transcona Sharks.

"Hey, Wiz."

Cody shook his head. Someone was calling him from the other end of the dressing room. Whoever it was had mouthed his new nickname with open disdain.

Cody opened his eyes abruptly. He looked across the room. Before him stood Stu Brackett. By now the rest of the players had all left.

"You're really getting on my nerves, you know," Stu spat out the words. He held his body tensely. Like he was ready to challenge Cody to a fight, Cody thought, but not quite.

"What are you talking about?" Cody asked.

"I'm talking about last practice when you tried to make me look bad, and today, scoring the winning goal." Cody noticed Stu's eyes were red and puffy, as if he'd just been crying. "I finally do something to get noticed by setting up the tying goal and then you come along and steal the glory."

Cody didn't know what to say. Of course he hadn't been trying to make Stu look bad, he'd just been doing his best. Stu must be jealous I scored the winning goal, Cody figured.

"I'm not looking for trouble," Cody said, awkwardly nudging his duffel bag with his feet.

"I think you are. You're trying to steal my spot."

"No, I'm not."

"And you're sucking up to my dad, too."

"No way, Stu, you're wrong," Cody protested.

Stu thumped his chest. "Just so long as you remember I'm the left winger on this team." With the toe of his boot, Stu struck Cody's duffel bag. The equipment inside shifted.

"You can't stop me from playing hockey," Cody replied. Just because he's the coach's son, Cody thought, does he think he can boss around everybody on the team? "I made this team fair and square."

"So did I," Stu went on. "And I had it tougher than everybody else. Because my dad's the coach, and he expects me to be that much better than everybody else." He turned and stalked out of the dressing room.

Suddenly, Cody understood how much playing on the Sharks meant to Stu. Way more than it means to me, even, Cody thought. And he had a good idea why. Stu just wanted to earn his dad's respect. Playing on the Sharks was Stu's way of reaching out to his dad.

Still, Cody reasoned, it wasn't his fault Stu's dad was so hard on him and expected so much. Stu shouldn't take it out on him.

Cody pulled on his shirt. Determined not to allow Stu's threats to ruin his enjoyment of his first day as a full-fledged Transcona Shark, he tried to replay in his mind the goal he'd scored only a few minutes ago. But it wasn't easy.

At that moment, a group of older boys from one of the teams playing in the next game walked into the dressing room. Cody dressed himself quickly, picked up his bag, and quietly walked out of the room.

The last thing he wanted right now was to ride in Coach Brackett's car along with Stu. He found the coach still talking with the scorekeeper and told him his mom was coming to pick him up. Then he walked outside into the cold December night and stood in a smelly bus shelter along with an old woman in a ragged overcoat, waiting for a bus to take him home. He dug his hands into his pockets and hoped he had enough change for the fare.

11

Just Like Old Times, Only Different

"Tell us all about it," Ryan asked.

"Every last detail," Mitch added.

It was the afternoon after Cody's first game with the Transcona Sharks, and he'd tramped to "the Igloo," hoping to find the boys there. After his encounter with Stu, he felt a need to see his old friends again.

"I wouldn't know where to start," Cody confided, lying back comfortably on Ernie's goalie pad. "It was really something."

"At recess today," Mitch said, "Noah Rivard told me that you scored the winning goal. That's showing them."

"Way to go," Ernie put in. "I knew you could hold up against those guys. I bet we all could."

Mitch lowered his glasses on his nose and eyeballed Ernie. "Maybe you guys could," he said. "But not me."

"You never know," Cody suggested.

"I have a pretty good idea." Mitch continued sorting a pile of hockey cards he'd brought with him. "I belong in the press box, not on the ice."

Cody smiled. It was a quiet, windless day, the sky clear and the air not overly cold.

"Were there lots of people in the stands?" Ryan asked.

"Hundreds," Cody answered. "And they cheered so loudly you could hardly hear yourself think."

"That must have been exciting," Ryan said.

"It was," Cody admitted. "You really get pumped up by all that noise. But I'll tell you something, a lot of those parents can really get nasty."

"What do you mean?" Mitch asked.

"Well, they really rag on you if you make a mistake," Cody explained. "Like one parent spent the whole night hollering, 'Wipe the fog off your glasses, kid!' to one player just because he missed a few passes."

"Did anybody take a crack like that at you?" Mitch asked.

"You bet," Cody confessed. He had to laugh. "When I was caught offside one time, one guy shouted that I should study the rule book a little better."

"The nerve!" Ernie exploded.

"How about the hitting?" Ryan enquired.

"You get hit almost every second you're on the ice. Everybody's moving so fast it would be impossible not to collide. In fact, one of the Elks knocked me so hard I fell on my butt."

Cody noticed Ryan wince at the thought of the collision, then catch himself and force his face back to normal.

"Did you knock him back?" Ernie asked.

"No, I didn't get the chance. You're not on the ice much, come to think of it. Each shift is only a few minutes."

"That's no fun," Ernie grumbled.

"Actually, the goalies usually play the whole game, so you'd be OK, Ernie," Cody said. "It's all the other players who take shifts."

"How'd you feel when you scored the goal?" Ryan asked.

"Great. But it happened so fast I can hardly remember it now."

Mitch was reading the statistics on the back of one his cards. "That's why you should have your dad videotaping you," he offered. "My dad always videotapes my brother's games."

The boys fell silent.

"Oh, sorry," Mitch said, looking at Cody contritely. "I guess I just forgot for a second."

Cody rose off the goalie pad. "It's OK," he said. Then he changed the subject. He would rather think about other things right now. "The pressure in a league game can sure be tough. I mean, the parents, the referee, the scorekeeper, the coach, your teammates — they're all watching your every move. If you make a mistake, no matter how small, it's like you've broken the law."

The boys shook their heads in digust.

"That's not right," Ryan said.

"It gets to be too much," Cody agreed. "I think most of the people at the game think we're playing in the NHL or something."

"Coach Brackett must be hard to take, huh?" Ernie asserted.

Cody hadn't known how, if at all, to bring up his problem with Stu, but this seemed like the right time.

"He's tough, all right," Cody said, "especially on his own son. It's like he's not satisfied with Stu unless Stu's the absolute best player on the team. And now Stu's so worked up he's mad at me because we both play left wing and Coach Brackett seems to be noticing me more than he notices Stu."

"Sounds like there could be trouble," Ryan offered.

"There already is," Cody confessed. "In the dressing room after the game, Stu came up to me and told me to stay out of his way, that he was the Transcona Sharks left winger and I'd better not forget that. He even kicked my duffel bag."

"I told you those guys were snooty jerks," Ernie huffed.

"I guess you were right," Cody remarked, "but — I don't know — somehow I feel sorry for Stu. It must be tough being ignored by your own dad."

As the words came out of his mouth, a thought struck Cody, like a pin dropping deep inside his mind. It must be tough on my dad, too, to be ignored by me. I wonder if I'm doing the right thing.

"So what are you going to do?" Mitch asked.

Cody was still thinking about his dad. When he heard Mitch's question it took him a few seconds to realize that Mitch was asking about the problem with Stu, not Cody's problem with his dad. He shook his head a moment, as if to clear his mind.

"I don't know," he answered. "I guess I'll just keep playing and hope things will work themselves out. What else can I do?"

"Show them you deserve to be on that team," Mitch insisted. "That's what."

In a while Ernie looked at his watch. "Hey, guys, it's already ten after six. We told Jeremy we'd meet him at six o' clock on the dot. Let's get going."

Mitch and Ryan joined Ernie in hurrying to their feet.

"Hey, where are you guys going?" Cody asked.

"To the rink," Ernie answered. "Jeremy's already there waiting for us."

"Oh," Cody said. For a moment he didn't understand why they hadn't asked him to play with them, but then he realized that, of course, they would have needed a replacement for him now that he'd joined the Sharks and wasn't always around.

Cody looked at Ryan. "I can go home and get your equipment, so you can play," he offered.

Ryan smirked. "It's all right," he said. "For the past week I've been playing without the equipment and I'm kind of getting used to it. It's fun."

"But you could get hurt," Cody insisted. "What would your parents say?"

Ernie patted Ryan on the back. "Don't worry about him," he told Cody. "He's already taken a few spills and bounced right back." He nodded to Ryan. "Show Cody that bruise on your arm."

Ryan slipped off his jacket and rolled up his sleeve, like a sailor showing off a tattoo. Sure enough, there was a black and blue bruise there the size of a Loonie.

"Ouch!" Cody exclaimed. "That must have hurt."

"It did," Ryan admitted. "But it's not so bad now." He rubbed it with his thumb. "I think I might even miss it when it's gone."

The boys laughed.

Then Cody was met by another surprise.

"Ernie, what are those?" he said pointing to a pair of worn hockey skates jutting out of Ernie's bag of goalie equipment.

"What do they look like to you, fool?" Ernie asked back, grinning. "They're hockey skates."

"I know that, *fool*," Cody said. "But you don't skate."

"Well, I'm starting to learn," Ernie explained. "It is about time, wouldn't you say? A guy can stay cramped up in the goalie crease only so long." He flashed a wide grin and mimed a skating motion. "It's time to roam around the rest of the rink."

Cody howled with delight.

"How about you," Cody said, pointing to Mitch. "Do you have any surprises for me?"

"Me?" Mitch mouthed. "No, not a thing. I'm still the klutz on skates I always was." Then he touched his index finger to his lips, like a TV detective about to reveal some new evidence. "Except one thing. I do get to score a few more goals now, playing with Jeremy rather than you. He's not half the puck hog you were." Mitch burst out laughing. "Just kidding! Just kidding!" he said.

Cody twisted Mitch's head into a play headlock. These guys are the best, he thought.

But part of him also wished he could have been in on all the fun they seemed to be having lately. Why'd they pick this week to make all these new changes?

The boys made their way out of "the Igloo," Ernie carefully placing a few branches over the plywood roof to further camouflage their secret hiding place. The four of them stood outside in the calm, cool air.

"I guess we'll see you later," Ryan said to Cody.

But Cody didn't have anywhere to go just then. He wished the guys would invite him to their hockey game. It would be nice to forget all about Stu and the Transcona Sharks for a while.

"Isn't anybody going to ask me to join you guys out on the rink?" he protested.

"We figured you might have a practice or something," Ryan explained.

"Well, I don't," Cody said.

"Hurry up, then," Ernie said. "Jeremy's waiting. Maybe we can call on Dale, too, and we can play three-on-three."

The boys had no time to use the narrow path they'd created walking to and from "the Igloo" just about every other day, so they cut across the field, stamping through deep drifts of snow.

It felt good, Cody thought, to be with the guys again. And it probably wouldn't feel too bad, either, to get back onto the outdoor rink.

12

All in the Family

Watch this," Cody announced to his mother and sister. He took the four pairs of socks he'd just folded into tight balls and tossed them into the air, trying to juggle them. One by one the socks tumbled to the basement floor.

His mom laughed. "Maybe you should stick to hockey, dear."

"Yeah," Tish added. "I don't think you'd make it as a trained seal."

It was laundry day at the Powell home. Cody and his mom and sister were in the basement, doing their best to work through three baskets brimming with dirty clothes. Tomorrow Cody and the Transcona Sharks were playing in Lord Strathcona Arena against the St. Vital Marauders. Christmas was only five days away.

Cody's mom wiped a line of sweat from her brow. "I don't know why I take days off," she said. "They're too tiring." She heaved the third loaded laundry basket onto the washing machine and started placing the dirty clothes inside. "A seven-day work week, huh? Maybe it's not such a bad idea."

"Mom, I'm still a little worried about leaving you and Cody alone for so long," Tish declared. Beside her on the ironing board, she'd neatly stacked three piles of folded T-shirts and underwear. "How will you manage to keep this house in order without my help?"

Cody's mom chuckled. "I don't know, honey, I honestly don't know." Her eyes travelled up and down Tish's neat stacks of clothes with obvious admiration. "Maybe I'll just insist that for that week Cody wears only one change of clothes, not his usual twenty-five."

"Very funny," Cody scoffed. He held up a pair of his jockey shorts. "Does that include underwear?"

Tish made a sickened face. Cody's mom tousled his hair affectionately.

"You two are coming to my game tomorrow night at Lord Strathcona, right?" Cody asked. He really wanted his mom and sister to see him in action as a Transcona Shark.

"Of course," his mom answered. "I know I'll be free." She looked down at Tish, smiling. "How about you, Tish? You won't be too busy tomorrow night will you? I mean, the bathroom is scrubbed clean, your bedroom closet has been organized ..."

"Mom!" Tish protested. Then she turned to Cody. "No, I wouldn't miss Cody's game for the world."

"Sounds like you'll have your very own cheering section, then," Cody's mom said. "Me, Tish, and your grandfather. He promised to come by tomorrow afternoon to fix the leaky faucet in the kitchen. When he finds out we're going to watch you play hockey, I'm sure he'll come along."

Yeah, Cody thought to himself, everybody will be there. Except my dad.

Cody's mom transferred some clean clothes to an empty laundry basket, which she then handed to Tish. "Honey, would you take this upstairs and start putting the clothes away in the drawers," she asked. "Cody and I'll be up in just a few minutes."

"OK, Mom," Tish said. She walked to the bottom of the stairs with the basket, nudged off her slippers and began the climb upstairs. Then she turned back. "Are we going to bring up the tree later and decorate it?" she asked, her head craned towards the laundry room.

"Why not?" Cody's mom replied. "If I can just convince Cody to help me haul up the tree and the boxes of decorations."

"Maybe tomorrow," Cody groaned. "I'm too tired today."

"But Christmas is only a few days away," Tish complained.

Cody's mom took a deep breath. "It's all right," she put in. "We can wait until Cody's up to it."

"I guess so," Tish said, hurrying up the stairs. Cody could hear the disappointment in her voice.

Wiping sweat from her forehead, Cody's mom returned to her chore. She sprinkled detergent over the load of laundry in the washing machine and closed the lid. Then she punched a few buttons and turned the timer on. The washing machine chugged into motion with a loud roar.

"That thing makes more noise than a diesel engine," she joked.

Cody folded the last pair of socks and tossed them into another laundry basket, hook shot style. "Can I be excused now?" he asked.

"Not quite yet," Cody's mom said. She led him by the shoulder to the lawn chair she'd set up for herself in the laundry room. "Have a seat. There's something I'd like to talk to you about."

Cody sat down.

"Cody, I want you to know that I think it's a good idea for you to visit your dad with Tish after Christmas."

Cody hung his head.

"I know you haven't been getting along with your dad since the divorce, but you've got to start trying. God knows, he's not one of my favourite people right now, but he deserves a chance from you. I've talked to him a few times since he called last week, and he really wants to see you."

Cody's mom knelt down next to him. She wiped a wisp of hair out of his eyes. "Cody, the one thing your dad and I *could* agree on when we separated was that we didn't want to get in each other's way when it came to you and Tish. Now that your dad's in Kamloops, holidays are probably the only time he'll be able to see you guys."

"Then why'd he move there?" Cody asked curtly.

"I don't know, Cody," his mom said. Her eyes were bleary. "But that's the way things have turned out. No matter what, though, he'll always be your dad." She kissed his cheek. "Promise me you'll think it over again. Please."

In that moment the washing machine boomed and banged, and actually hurled itself forward a few centimetres, like a monster coming to life in an old horror movie. Cody was thankful for the interruption. He couldn't make any promises to his mother right now.

Cody's mom bounced back up, unable to hold back a spurt of nervous laughter upon witnessing the washing machine's slow crawl along the basement floor.

"Help me move this thing back into place, would you, Cody?"

Together Cody and his mom shoved the machine back against the wall.

Cody's mom slapped the dust off her hands and took a deep breath. "You know, this washing machine, along with the dryer, was a wedding present for your dad and me from both our parents. And the very first time I used it, it did exactly what you just saw." She paused. "Maybe I should have taken that as a sign of how things were going to work out," she cracked, smiling.

Cody smiled as best he could back at her. "Can I be excused now?" he asked again.

"No problem," his mom answered.

Cody ran upstairs. There was so much to think about, so much to try to sort out, he didn't know where to begin. Why does everything have to be so complicated? he thought. He decided all he wanted to do right now was lie down in his bed, play some music real loud, and stare up at the ceiling.

When he entered the bedroom, though, he found Tish there, still putting away some clothes. As well, a little cloth suitcase she liked to call her own was open on her bed, half filled with clothes.

"What are you doing?" Cody asked.

"What does it look like I'm doing? I'm packing," Tish answered.

As tiny as the bedroom was, Cody and Tish had managed to split it into two very distinctive halves. On Cody's side, posters of hockey and basketball players plastered the walls, and clothes were strewn about messily. On Tish's side, everything was neatly folded and put away, and on the night table there was a leatherbound Bible bracketed by a framed photograph taken the last time all four members of the family had spent Christmas together.

"Packing?" Cody repeated. "For what?"

"For the trip to Kamloops."

Cody couldn't help laughing. "Don't you think it's a little early? You've still got six days."

"I like to be organized," Tish responded. She returned to what she had been doing a few moments ago: arranging her T-shirts into different piles, separated by colour, so she'd have an easier time choosing which ones she would take with her.

"Organized is one thing," Cody joked, "but you, little sis, are crazy." Then he twirled his index finger beside his head in the cuckoo motion.

Tish sniffled, and Cody could tell he'd hurt her. Immediately, he regretted his crack.

"I'm sorry," he said, moving across the bedroom to her side. "Let me help you pack."

"Sure," Tish answered. Her head was still down. She moved to the bureau and leaned down to open the bottom drawer. "How many pairs of pants do you think I'll need?"

"I don't know," Cody answered. He was absently adding more T-shirts to the suitcase. Then, suddenly, he pulled something out of the pocket along the top of the case. It was a folded newspaper page.

"What's this?" he asked, unfolding the page and taking a look at it himself. He didn't need to wait for Tish's answer. Immediately, he recognized the article that had appeared that week in the *Transcona Views*, reporting on the Sharks victory over the Elks. There was a small picture of some of the players, including Cody, in the top-right corner of the page.

"I wanted to show the article to Dad," Tish explained. She moved to grab it from Cody, but he stopped her.

"He wouldn't be interested," Cody said.

"Yes, he would," Tish insisted.

For a moment Cody considered keeping the article himself and hiding it away somewhere so Tish couldn't take it with her to Kamloops. But then he thought that maybe she was right, maybe his dad would be interested. And then, in the next moment, he told himself, of course, Dad would be interested in seeing this article. It would make him proud and he'd remember all the times we used to practise together in the back yard. Cody neatly refolded the page and replaced it in the pocket of the suitcase.

Tish smiled. Cody couldn't help admiring his little sister then. For a seven-year-old girl, he admitted, she sure was certain of everything she did and believed in.

Brother and sister resumed packing the suitcase, and soon they were done. As Cody moved to his side of the room to finally lie down, Tish followed him and sat down next to him on the bed.

"Are you still sure you don't want to come with me?" Tish asked Cody.

"Yes," Cody answered. But, he realized, all of a sudden he wasn't so sure at all. "I already went through all this downstairs with Mom."

"But I'm afraid to travel by myself on the train," Tish said.

"You have nothing to worry about," Cody said. "The stewards love having kids to take care of. They'll treat you like a princess."

Tish sniffled again and bit her lower lip, as if she were holding something back, something deep inside her.

"I'm so afraid of going there alone," she said. She was looking away from Cody.

Cody rubbed the back of her neck, his face next to hers. "I told you, you'll be OK. The ride there'll be a blast."

"That's not what I mean," Tish sobbed. She was looking directly at Cody now. "I'm afraid of how it'll be with Dad and his new family." A single tear emerged from the corner of her right eye, like a miniature bubble. "Please come with me, Cody."

"I can't," he said.

"Why not?" she pleaded.

He couldn't explain it to her, because, he realized, he couldn't explain it to himself.

"Just because," he said.

"Will Dad still love me, Cody? Will he love me as much as he loves his new kids?" Tish was crying openly now, not fighting it back at all. Cody felt the wetness of her tears on his cheeks.

"Of course he will," he found himself saying. "He's our dad, Tish, he'll always love us."

Now he was holding her in his arms. He felt her shaking. He was scared. This was the first time since the divorce that he had seen his sister cry, really cry, at something serious, something having to do with their family, not some TV show.

"Why'd this happen to us, Cody?" Tish pleaded. It was the question Cody had asked himself every day since his mom and dad had separated, but it was the first time he had heard it from Tish's lips.

"I don't know," he said. He hugged Tish tightly. "But don't worry. We'll make the best of it."

13

Hockey Night in Transcona

As he laced on his skates, Cody kept his eyes glued to Coach Brackett's chalkboard, which showed the various lines and circles of a hockey rink. He didn't want to miss one word of the coach's instructions.

"The Marauders are a strong, experienced team," the coach explained. He printed MARAUDERS in thick block letters over one end of his chalkboard. "In goal, they've got McDowell." He looked down at the sheet of paper on his clipboard. "Quick hands, but he has a tendency to leave a tiny hole between his pads." Then the coach marked off the Marauders defencemen. "Look for Pilski on defence," he said. "You won't miss him, because he'll be the biggest guy on the ice. Whatever you do, don't try to outmuscle him. He'll beat you every time. Try some finesse." Coach Brackett pointed to Cody. "Wiz, that's where I expect your stickhandling to come in handy. Don't disappoint me."

Cody gulped and felt his stomach tighten. All of a sudden, he wasn't so sure how much he liked playing under pressure.

"As for their forwards," Coach Brackett continued, "watch out for Danko." He paced the floor of the dressing room, his heels clicking ominously. "He's lightning fast, and I've heard he could score goals in this league with his eyes closed and one arm tied behind his back. Let's not let something like that happen tonight."

The players looked at each other with worried eyes. Each of them, Cody noticed, was dressing himself slowly and carefully, as if a wrong move now — taping a stick a little off centre, missing a loop while lacing on shoulder pads — might indicate worse things yet to come.

"I want you all to play hard. Intensity's the name of the game." The coach grabbed a hockey stick standing up against the wall and flicked it hard a few times with his wrists, as if he wished he could skate onto the ice himself and help the team win this game. "Come the spring, I have a strong suspicion the Marauders are the team we're going to have to beat if we want to make the city finals. Tonight let's prove that we're capable of doing just that."

Cody finally finished with his skates. He estimated that he'd probably tied and retied the laces of each skate about twenty times.

Coach Brackett picked up his clipboard again. "I'm not changing much from our first game," he announced. "The Line One forwards will still be Travis, Kurt, and Stu, and on Line Two I've kept Derrick, Noah, and Cody."

As the coach rattled off the rest of the lineup, Cody sighed with relief. Even though the Line One players usually earned more ice time, he was much happier playing on Line Two. For one thing, the pressure would be a little less hectic. For another, he wouldn't have to deal with Stu accusing him of stealing his spot.

Cody knew how important it was to play well tonight. To help the team win, of course, but for so many other reasons, as well. His mom, Tish, and his grandfather, and Ryan, Mitch, and Ernie would all be in the stands watching the game, rooting him on. He wanted to give them something to cheer about. He also wanted to prove to Stu that, whether Stu liked it or not, Cody was a valuable member of this team. And, more than anything else, he wanted to prove to himself that he had deserved a spot on the Transcona Sharks all along.

Cody thought back to about half an hour ago when he'd walked up the flight of stairs to the front hall of Lord Strathcona Arena, his duffel bag full of equipment banging against his side. He'd been extremely nervous, but proud, too, as if he'd finally made it big, as if he'd finally done something that deserved notice. Then, as he walked inside, he'd been totally awed by the rows of trophies and team pictures displayed in an enormous wooden case opposite the canteen. He'd wondered what it would feel like to have his picture displayed in that case, or to take home one of those trophies for just a week to show it to all his friends and to his mom and to his dad.

He'd like to be able to do that.

Abruptly, Cody returned his thoughts to the game ahead. He silently repeated Coach Brackett's instructions, reminding himself of everything he was expected to do tonight. The last thing he wanted was to make any mistakes.

"OK, men," Coach Brackett called out. His eyes seemed to be smouldering. "Let's hit the ice."

The boys finished dressing and marched out of the dressing room in single file, their skate blades clanging against the cement flooring of the passageway leading to the ice.

The arena was filled with fans, entire families sitting or standing on the rows of stands climbing all the way up to the rafters. To Cody, it seemed that all of Transcona had shown up for tonight's game. As he approached the gate that led to the ice, he took a series of deep breaths. Then he pushed off, right foot forward, onto the smooth ice surface of Lord Strathcona Arena. His head was spinning with excitement.

Out on the ice, Cody took a few long strides to warm up, then bent his legs at the knees, one at a time, stretching them back with his hands all the way to his butt. A thin mist rose from the ice, lending the arena a dreamlike quality. Cody closed his eyes and tried to collect his thoughts.

When he opened his eyes again, he decided to take a closer look through the stands. High over the home bench he found his mom, Tish, and his grandfather. As they noticed him looking up at them, they waved to him. He nodded his head underneath the plastic helmet to acknowledge their greeting.

Then he spotted Ryan and Ernie standing just behind the near net, their noses actually touching the Plexiglas over the boards. He skated towards them. Where's Mitch? he wondered. In the next second, a head popped up from beneath the boards. Sure enough, it was Mitch, a video camera perched over his shoulder.

"Smile, you're on *Candid Camera*," Mitch kidded, shouting so Cody could hear him. The little red light on the side of the camera started blinking. "My dad let me use this tonight. I'll be doing the play-by-play myself."

Cody chuckled. Then he turned back. He skated to the centre of the ice and picked up a puck. He ran through some of his favourite stickhandling moves, then fired a shot at the goalie, Eddie, who kicked it to the boards with his pad. Cody continued skating. The more he skated, he found, the less nervous he felt.

By now the Marauders had taken the ice. Cody eyed them closely, without being too obvious. Draped in their black and silver uniforms, the Marauders players appeared huge to him. They seemed to move across the ice, fast and orderly, like bees buzzing to and from a hive. The inside of Cody's stomach took a few more flip-flops.

In no time, the referee blasted his whistle and called for the opening face-off. One by one, each of the Sharks players skated to their goaltender and patted him on the right shoulder, for good luck. As Cody had been informed earlier by Travis, the tap had to be on the right shoulder, and made only once. Then everyone except the Line One players skated off the ice and over to the home bench.

Taking a seat beside his linemates, Derrick and Noah, Cody gazed up at the electronic scoreboard. HOME 0, VISITORS 0, it read. He wondered how long that would last.

By the looks of it, the Marauders were just as eager to win this game as the Sharks. Their players forechecked and back-checked, and hustled up and down the length of the ice when-ever the puck changed hands. Cody followed the speedy movements of the forwards in particular. Together they attacked the Sharks zone like waves crashing onto a beach.

Towards the end of the first shift, as Kurt began a rush on the right wing into the Marauders zone, Travis to his left, Stu wide on the opposite wing, it looked like the Sharks might be able to put something together. But then Kurt came face-to-face with Pilski. The massive defenceman simply moved into Kurt's path. Much like a brick wall. Kurt fell to the ice like a swatted fly. Then Pilski snagged the loose puck and cleared it quickly to Danko. That Pilski would not be an easy player to get past, Cody thought.

Puck in tow, Danko picked up speed, his upper body low to the ice. From behind his helmet, a tuft of blonde hair blew in the current of wind created by his swift movement. Now that's a hockey player, Cody thought.

As he crossed the centre line, Danko switched the puck from his forehand to his backhand, confusing the Sharks de-fender, then zipped a short pass to his forward. The forward took in the puck, twirled to his left, crossed the blue line, and returned the puck to Danko, who leaned down and fired, the only thing between him and the Sharks net the heavily padded body of Eddie Bruska and two metres of thin air.

The puck rose off the ice like an airplane taking off from a runway. Eddie shot out his glove hand, missing the puck by a few centimetres. A sure goal, Cody thought. But then the puck continued to rise. It pinged against the goalpost, a ringing sound echoing through the arena.

The rebound fell to Stu's stick. He cleared the puck with all his might. It was icing, but at least the Sharks had somehow managed to stop the Marauders drive.

On the bench Coach Brackett wrapped his arms against his chest and shook his head. "We have to play better than this," he muttered. "Line Two, get out there."

At the next whistle, Cody and his linemates charged onto the ice. Cody felt a heavy weight pressing down on him all the way from the roof of the arena. The bright lights, the noise from the fans, and the pressure all contributed to somehow freezing his muscles. He banged his head a few times through Ryan's helmet. There was no way he was going to let himself crack under this pressure.

"Don't even dream about making the finals this year, buddy," the Marauders forward across from Cody for the face-off snarled at him, "because you'll never get past us."

Cody dug his skates into the ice and waited, saying nothing back. I'll prove myself on the ice, he thought.

In a few seconds the play moved deep into the Marauders end. Cody chased the puck, his legs moving like pistons. A Marauders defenceman held possession, but couldn't seem to find an open forward to pass to. Play physical, Cody repeated to himself. He lunged for the puck with his stick, determined to strip it from the Marauders player. Suddenly, and for no apparent reason, the Marauders player's feet swung into the air in front of him and he collapsed onto the ice like a felled tree. Cody pounced on the loose puck and looked up for an open player.

At the same moment the referee's whistle shrilled loudly.

"Tripping, two minutes," the referee called out, pointing to Cody.

"He's faking!" Cody protested. "I didn't even touch him."

"Sorry, son, but I have to call what I see."

"That kid deserves an Academy Award," Derrick blurted.

The referee ignored Derrick and escorted Cody to the penalty box. As the gate closed behind him, locking him away from the action, Cody looked with pleading eyes towards Coach Brackett. He hoped the coach realized that he had had nothing to do with the penalty, that the Marauders player had obviously taken the dive to draw a penalty.

But, like the referee, Coach Brackett had been fooled by the Marauders player's act. On the bench he was fuming. His black moustache was slick with sweat. "We can't be taking stupid penalties in a game like this!" he cried out. He crunched the can of pop he held in his hands and flung it into the garbage can behind the bench.

From the penalty box, Cody shook his head in disbelief. He couldn't believe what had just happened. These Marauders were not only good hockey players, he thought, they were also sly. Cody wished he could just close his eyes, and when he opened them again his two-minute penalty would be over. But it wasn't going to be that easy. Coach Brackett sent out the Sharks penalty-killing squad. Somehow they had to stop the Marauders power play. Cody prayed they would.

The Marauders power play was lifted right out of a hockey textbook. Danko penetrated deep, flitting dangerously about the Sharks net, while Pilski and his partner on defence set themselves up at the two points just inside the blue line.

The puck came to Pilski at the point. He directed a pass to Danko, who rushed the net, trying to somehow thrust the puck past the goal line. The goalie stood tall, then leaned forward and poked the puck free. He was in fine form tonight, Cody thought. Then Stu took the puck and skated wide. He knew he had to clear the puck far down the ice so he lifted his stick high to work up more power. But as he came down to swing at the puck, his blade fanned. Danko stole the loose puck and passed back to Pilski.

With not a single Sharks player daring to attempt a block, Pilski took all the time in the world to set up for a slapshot. His stick met the puck with a thunderous clapping sound. The puck sailed untouched all the way to the goalie, who somehow halted its course with his blocker. But Danko picked up the rebound and lifted the puck over the goalie's shoulder into the upper-right corner of the net.

Marauders 1, Sharks 0.

The power play over, Cody returned to the Sharks bench. So did the penalty-killing team, while Line Three skated onto the ice.

"How could you have muffed that clearing shot, Stu?" Coach Brackett roared. "You don't just close your eyes and try to take a whack at the puck. You play it carefully, making sure of the play."

"Sorry, Dad," Stu appealed. "I was just trying to ..."

"No excuses, please!" The coach turned away from his son. "Excuses don't win hockey games."

Cody cringed. He felt awful. His penalty, bogus or not, had allowed the Marauders the opportunity to score the first goal of the game and also put Stu in a tight spot with his dad. He thought of saying something to Stu, but knew that he was probably the last person on earth Stu wanted to talk to right now. If it were possible, Cody thought, he wouldn't mind suddenly disappearing.

But it wasn't possible. Cody sat on the bench and watched the action, as Line Three of the Sharks tried to stave off the Marauders attack. But the momentum garnered from the power-play goal just seemed to build, and twenty seconds later another Marauders forward pierced the Sharks defensive blockade and netted a goal.

The Marauders held a two-goal lead.

The home fans inside Lord Strathcona Arena were hushed. On the bench the players wagged their heads in disgust. Coach Brackett kicked the boards in front of him and shouted angry instructions to the players out on the ice.

After a few more ineffectual shifts for Lines One and Two, the buzzer finally blared, signalling the end of the first period.

The scoreboard read, HOME 0, VISITORS 2.

The Marauders strutted off the ice. Meanwhile, as they took their seats on the home-team bench, the Sharks players speared their sticks in front of them and hung their heads.

Behind two goals to the strongest team in the league, the Transcona Sharks knew their chances of winning this game were not very good.

14

The Pressure Builds

Coach Brackett slammed the gate hard behind the last player off the ice.

"I have half a mind to send all of you guys on your sweet way home and call the B squad to get down here and take over," he growled. "The way you're playing is pitiful."

The players squirted water into their mouths, wiped their heads with towels, retied their skates. Most of them just grunted and nodded to one another. Nobody said so much as a word.

"Are we going to turn this game around or not?" Coach Brackett asked.

"We can do it," the boys answered.

"What's that?" the coach asked. His voice was booming. "I couldn't quite hear you."

"We can do it!" the boys shouted in unison.

"That's what I like to hear!" The coach pounded the heel of his hands against the top of the boards. "I know you guys are capable of pulling this off, if you really want to."

Again the boys shouted, "We can do it!"

Coach Brackett paced up and down the length of the narrow bench.

"I'm going to be making some changes over the next two periods," he said, "so I want all of you to be playing close attention. I'll be switching lines around, mixing and matching, trying to get something started."

The buzzer blared again to begin the second period.

"The forwards I want to see out there right now are Travis, Kurt, and Cody," Coach Brackett hollered. He windmilled his right arm, hurrying the boys onto the ice. "Get out there, men, and score some goals. Remember to press the net."

Cody was stunned. He'd been promoted to the first line. He couldn't wait to see what he could do playing with Travis and Kurt. At the same time, though, he felt bad for Stu, whom he'd replaced. As he stepped onto the ice, he noticed Stu glaring at him with hateful eyes.

Travis won the face-off and the Sharks pushed ahead into the opposing zone. Immediately, they picked up the pace, taking the game right to the Marauders. Like it or not, Cody admitted, Coach Brackett's angry words had fired up the team.

Crossing the blue line, Travis passed to Kurt. Kurt deked around a Marauders defender and snapped a shot on net. Wide. The puck caromed off the boards behind the net and onto Cody's stick.

Cody picked up the puck. It was time to concentrate on his specialty, he decided. Stickhandling. He skated ahead, dribbling the puck back and forth with the blade of his stick. Pilski approached him, but Cody shoulder-faked and slipped around him. That wasn't too hard, he thought, smiling to himself. Suddenly, the sheer exhilaration of skating and stickhandling returned to him. He could sense that something good was going to happen soon.

In front of him, the Marauders goalie had the net covered, so Cody opted against shooting and slipped to temporary safety behind the net. From there he looked out towards his teammates. With a goal scorer's homing instincts, Kurt was charging towards the net. Quickly, Cody flicked the puck towards him. Kurt caught the puck and set up for a wrist shot. From such a close distance, and with the goalie screened, Cody knew Kurt was sure to score.

Bang!

Pilski blasted into Kurt, smashing him into the goalpost and lifting the net off its bearings. Instantly, a whistle was blown. In the next second, though, Travis reached the puck and sent it cruising into the uprooted net.

The Sharks players lifted their sticks in celebration.

But the referee was waving his hands frantically in front of his chest. "No goal! No goal!" he repeated. "The shot was made after the whistle was blown. A two-minute roughing penalty on the Marauders defenceman, but no goal!"

Travis flew after the referee, begging him to change his mind, but the referee kept shaking his head. The fans were on their feet, booing the call. Meanwhile, Coach Brackett, with almost his entire body leaning over the bench, cried out for a penalty shot.

"Can't be done," the referee claimed. "There's just no reason."

"But we had a sure goal!" Coach Brackett insisted.

"That's your opinion, Coach," the referee explained. "Not mine."

"Maybe you need a pair of glasses then, buddy," Coach snarled.

The referee skated to Coach Brackett. "Coach, I'm warning you to stop arguing." He was shouting, even though his nose was almost touching Coach Brackett's. "Or I'll have to throw you out of the game. The call has been made. Let's get on with the game."

The referee then skated away and instructed the players to gather for a face-off to the right of the Marauders net. At the same time, to shore up the power-play attack, Coach Brackett pulled one of his defencemen off the ice and replaced him with an extra forward. The players waited as the forward took the ice. Cody looked up from his crouched position and saw that it was Stu Brackett.

In the next instant, the referee dropped the puck. Travis won the face-off, backhanding it to a Sharks player waiting at the point. The player faked the slapshot and snuck forward, pulling a Marauders defenceman out of position.

"I'm open!" Cody called.

The puck came to him, and without stopping he gathered it in and motored towards the net. Flustered, the Marauders defence cracked, skating off without rhyme or reason into different directions. Cody saw an open path straight in front of him. As well, to Cody's left, Stu skated in a tight circle, dangerously close to the Marauders net.

Cody didn't know whether to continue his charge on net or pass to Stu. He knew he had to make up his mind quickly or the Marauders defence would once again close up. He decided to trust his gut. Without thinking, he found himself shuffling a short pass to Stu. Stu's face showed momentary surprise, and then he leaned down and one-timed the puck straight at the net. Blindly, the goalie whipped out his glove hand. The puck nicked the stitching on the end of the glove and deflected wide.

Cody forced his way into the scrum of players in front of the net, found the puck, and chopped it over the goalie's outstretched leg.

The Sharks had scored their first goal!

From the stands Cody heard the thunderous boom of stamping feet.

"Great goal!" Travis exclaimed, showering Cody with pats on the helmet. Other players followed, joining the celebration. Then Stu skated into the circle of players. Cody didn't know what to expect from him. Awkwardly, Stu brushed his hand against Cody's shoulder.

"Way to play," he said. As if to indicate he meant what he was saying, he nodded his head twice.

"Thanks," Cody replied. Now he was sure that Stu was not a bad guy. All along, he'd just wanted his dad to pay some attention to him. And Cody could understand that. Very well.

Coach Brackett had no right to be so hard on Stu, Cody decided then. Why couldn't he just accept him for what he was?

Cody took his spot on the bench. He looked up at the rafters of the arena and for the first time noticed that they were decorated with multicoloured Christmas lights. He remembered that he still hadn't brought up the Christmas tree from the basement. Suddenly, he couldn't help wondering what kind of Christmas he was going to have this year.

Over the next few minutes, the Marauders regrouped and managed to slow down the pace of the game. Each team took turns moving the puck up the ice and then retreating when the opposing team closed off the lanes to the net. The second period closed with the score, Marauders 2, Sharks 1.

After another pep talk from Coach Brackett, the Sharks took the ice for the third period. They knew they had to press hard in order to score another goal, but the Marauders were playing cautious, defensive hockey. As soon as the Sharks forwards crossed the blue line, the Marauders defence would tighten up to form an impenetrable wall.

Late in the third period, with the clock threatening to drop the curtain on the Sharks comeback efforts, Coach Brackett sent out Travis, Cody, and Stu as his forward line, urging them to forecheck and force the puck loose from the powerful Marauders defence.

"Make something happen!" he hollered from the bench. "Come on, boys, hustle!"

Cody heeded the coach's command. He stuck like glue to Danko, the Marauders player controlling the puck, poking his stick out for the steal. But Danko protected the puck like a kid not about to share his candy bar. Obviously, the Marauders merely wanted to let the clock run down.

"We have to work together," Stu shouted from across the ice. In the next instant, taking a chance, Stu left the player he was covering and skated towards Cody and Danko. He kept his stick low to the ice to prevent a quick pass from Danko to the forward he'd just left open. Then, moving alongside Cody, he helped his teammate corner Danko in the neutral zone.

Danko bullied himself back into position, trying to freeze the puck against the boards with his skates. But Cody and Stu persisted with their poking and prodding at the puck, like two wasps buzzing around an open jar of honey. Stu lunged suddenly for the puck, and as Danko fended off the advance, Cody reached in with his stick and managed to tap the puck away slightly. Quickly, Stu straightened his body to form an obstacle to Danko. Meanwhile, Cody squirmed around the burly Marauders defenceman and seized the puck, managing to get enough wood on it to whack it across the ice towards Travis. All of a sudden, the Sharks scoring ace was on a breakaway.

Cody and Stu watched as Travis flew towards the Marauders net, building up speed with every stride, the closest Marauders defender at least two metres behind him. Expertly, Travis teased the puck in front of him from side to side and then, following Coach Brackett's pre-game advice, directed a wrist shot right between the goalie's legs. The puck squeezed through his pads and into the net like a squirrel darting into a hole in the ground.

The crowd went wild. Again, the sound of hundreds of pairs of boots stamping the floor filled the arena.

Cody looked up at the scoreboard. HOME 2, VISITORS 2, it read now. On the clock: 01:33. More than enough time, Cody thought, for the Marauders to score another goal and win the game. But also enough time for the Sharks to do the same. The outcome of this game was still very much up in the air.

"Way to forecheck," Stu called out to Cody.

"You, too," Cody replied, unsnapping his chin strap. The two boys, along with Travis, were moving towards the bench for the line change.

But Coach Brackett waved them back. "Stay out there for another shift, boys," he said. "I don't want to lose the momentum right now. We can still win this one!"

The boys grinned at each other and headed back to centre ice for the face-off. Cody could feel the adrenalin pumping through his veins. This is the kind of rush, he thought, that you just can't get playing two-on-two hockey on an outdoor rink. This is the real thing. League hockey. He leaned down on his stick, ready for the face-off.

The referee dropped the puck. Instantly, the Marauders centre muscled the puck from Travis and sent a pass to his left wing. Cody backtracked, his eyes fastened on the Marauders forwards as they pressed into the Sharks zone. Defending against as strong a group of players as the Marauders was not going to be easy.

The Marauders sharpshooters set themselves up inside the Sharks blue line. Obviously, like the Sharks, they were not content to settle for a tie. They passed the puck among themselves, looking for any holes in the Sharks defence. So far, though, there were none. Cody tensed, nervously waiting for the Marauders to make the next move. He felt a cold shiver as a trickle of sweat ran down his spine.

Finally, a Marauders forward decided to test the Sharks defensive wall. He darted towards the net along the right wing. Without hesitation, Cody and Stu descended upon him. Now we're really working like teammates, Cody thought. But the forward kept control of the puck, wheeling suddenly away from the boards and towards the net.

As the Marauders forward approached him, Cody, with Stu as his side, poked out his stick and felt it knock against the puck. His heart beat wildly with excitement and anticipation. Suddenly he sensed he could steal the puck and set up another breakaway like the one that had tied the game only a few seconds ago.

"I got it! I got it!" Cody called out to Stu as his stick hooked the puck away from the Marauder. "Move up for the pass!"

For a split second Stu stood frozen, unwilling to move out of his defensive position. Then, as he saw Cody bear down on the puck to make the leading pass, he bolted forward.

But the pass never came. Using his superior strength, the Marauders forward retrieved the puck from off Cody's stick and made a pass back to his centre man, who was perched in front of the Sharks net. Stu was caught at least five paces up ice. Cody, too, was behind the play. The Marauders centre had a clean shot on net.

As the centre set up for the shot, Cody held his breath. If the Marauders scored now, he was to blame. He alone.

The shot slammed off the centre's stick, headed directly for the upper right-hand corner of the net. Sweat poured down Cody's forehead and into his eyes. He had to strain to follow the course of the shot. It looked like a sure goal. But at the last second Eddie snapped his glove hand out and snatched the puck out of the air like a lizard's tongue catching a fly. And even though a horde of Marauders toppled towards him, Eddie held on tightly to the puck. The whistle blew. Cody sighed with relief.

The scoreboard remained unchanged. Except for the time. Now the clock read, 00:52. Less than a minute left to decide the fate of the game.

In the meantime, a young Sharks fan had thrown a cup of pop onto the ice to celebrate Eddie's save, so now the referee called a timeout in order to wipe up the mess. Coach Brackett screamed at his players to return to the bench immediately. From the look on the coach's face, Cody could tell that he did not want to leave this building tonight with a mere tie, no matter what it cost.

"If you guys would only play heads-up hockey out there, we could win this one," he roared.

The Sharks players hung their heads solemnly and snuck a few sips from their water bottles. Coach Brackett stormed up and down the bench. When he reached Stu, he stopped.

"As for you, Stu, what's the idea leaving your man so that you can start an offensive drive when our team doesn't even have control of the puck yet?" His face was livid. "That was a pretty stupid thing to do!"

"But Dad," Stu protested weakly, "it wasn't my ..."

"I told him to ..." Cody began to add.

"I don't want to hear any excuses!" Coach Brackett fumed. "We almost lost the game on that botch-up."

Cody watched as Stu moved to the edge of the bench. He took off his helmet and held his face in his hands, shaking it from side to side. Cody wished there was something he could do or say to make Stu feel better. But what?

Coach Brackett continued speaking. "There are fifty-two seconds left on the clock, boys. We can still win this one."

Cody wiped his face with a towel and looked up at the coach. He listened closely, hanging on the coach's every word. He knew how important an intelligent strategy for the final minute was, and he also knew that if anyone could instruct the Sharks how to win this game it was Coach Brackett. He realized suddenly that he probably wanted to win this game just as badly as the coach did.

"You have to press, press, and keep on pressing," Coach Brackett concluded, "until the puck's in the net." His eyes blazed. "Their net, that is."

Just then the referee whistled for the play to resume.

The coach quickly scanned some notes he'd scribbled onto the paper on his clipboard. "Here's the line-up," he announced.

Suddenly, the bench was hushed. Every boy on the bench looked up at the coach, eyes full of expectation, waiting to see who would be called upon to play the final fifty-two seconds. Cody's heart beat like a jackhammer.

"I want the same line-up on defence," the coach announced, "with Travis, Kurt, and Cody up front."

Cody was thrilled to have been chosen to play the final minute of the game, but at the same time he couldn't help being bothered that Stu had been excluded. Coach Brackett shouldn't have done that, he thought, not to his own son. It just wasn't right. Stu deserved a spot out on the ice right now. He'd played well tonight, Cody knew, and if anybody had botched up the last play it was him, not Stu.

Cody turned then to look down the bench at Stu. His head was bent low and his shoulders were heaving. Cody had no difficulty guessing that Stu was crying. A sick feeling crept through his stomach. He wished once again that there was something that he could do.

"Let's go, men," Coach Brackett called out. As Cody rose to follow Kurt down the bench and to the ice, the sick feeling in his stomach would not go away.

15

Hockey Hero

Coach Brackett held open the gate, as the players stepped down onto the ice. Last in line, Cody hesitated a second and then pushed off.

As his right foot hit the ice, the blade of his skate seemed to slip from beneath him, his ankle twisted outward at an apparently painful angle, and Cody collapsed.

He grabbed his ankle and shouted with pain, writhing on the ice. Coach Brackett jumped to his side.

"Are you all right, Cody?"

"No," he cried out between clenched teeth. "I've twisted my ankle."

Cody hoped his performance had been believable. He contorted his face as best he could into a mask of pain and kept clutching at his ankle. If the Marauders player could pull off a fake injury earlier, why couldn't he?

The referee gestured frantically at Coach Brackett to send out a replacement player so the game could continue. Just as Cody had hoped, the coach waved Stu onto the ice. Then he hurriedly lifted Cody over the boards and onto the bench.

Cody was relieved that he'd gotten away with his little acting stunt. Stu deserved this chance out on the ice right now, that much Cody was sure about.

Instantly, the puck was dropped and play resumed. As a parent tended to Cody's ankle, Coach Brackett turned to the action.

"Your ankle appears to be fine," the parent told Cody. "But it could swell on you." He handed Cody a bag of ice, which Cody applied to his ankle. The ice was cold, but the discomfort was worth the trouble, Cody thought. He stood up on his left foot, and watched Stu join the rest of the Sharks as they battled with the Marauders for possession of the puck in the neutral zone. As much as he'd wanted to play, he knew he'd made the right decision. His stomach felt better now.

The arena was noisy with cheering. Most of the fans and all of the players on both benches were standing on their feet, rooting for their teams. The excitement in the arena seemed almost to lift Cody off his feet.

At centre ice, Pilski tried to freeze the puck against the boards, but a Sharks defender poked it free. Noah dashed at the loose puck and whacked it forward towards the Marauders blue line.

Accelerating rapidly, Travis appeared to be able to reach the puck and make a move on net, but at the last second Danko materialized out of nowhere, beating Travis to the puck and swirling around in the opposite direction to begin a Marauders counterattack.

But he didn't count on Stu anticipating the play perfectly. As Danko faced forward, he found Stu braced directly in front of him. Trying to swerve around Stu, Danko lost his balance and the puck veered off his stick. Stu leaned in, picked up the puck, and skated forward, on a two-on-one breakaway with Travis.

Anybody in the arena who'd still been seated now rose to join the rest of the sea of standing fans. Coach Brackett was smiling widely, arms dancing at his sides. "You can do it, son! You can do it!"

Cody glanced at the time clock: 00:12, it read. Then he returned his eyes to the ice. With Travis to his right, Stu was descending on the Marauders net, a flash of turquoise and grey.

"Go, Stu!" Cody shouted.

The Marauders defender stuck with Stu, trying to force him wide, away from the net. Bearing down, Stu held the puck close to his body. By now he was about a metre from the net. It looked like he was going to try the shot himself. The defender fell to his knees. Then, at the last possible second, Stu lifted the puck and passed it back to Travis.

Travis had a clear shot on net. He switched the puck to his backhand and fired. At the same moment, the Marauders goalie flopped onto the ice in front of him.

The puck shot off Travis's stick. Then, suddenly, it was lost. Everyone in the arena — players, coaches, fans, and referee — seemed to crane their necks to find the puck. On his butt, the goaltender twisted and turned, desperately searching for the little black disk.

Then, in a burst of speed, Stu swooped to the net. The puck had trickled through the goalie's pads and was now motionless behind him, a mere hair's width from the goal line.

"Turn around!" the Marauders shouted to their goalie. He reached back with his glove at the evasive disk.

At the same moment, though, Stu hurled himself over the Marauders goalkeeper. With a sharp flick of the wrist, he buried the puck deep into the mesh of the net.

The goal light flashed on.

Cody turned to the electronic scoreboard: 00:00, the time clock read. Above it: HOME 3, VISITORS 2.

The crowd went crazy, practically lifting the roof off the arena. As the Marauders players shook their heads in disbelief, the Sharks on the bench, Cody included, stampeded onto

the ice to join in the celebration with the rest of their teammates, Coach Brackett right behind them. Cody didn't even
stop to consider if anyone would notice that he was suddenly
no longer limping.

Cody reached Stu. "Great goal!" he shouted, hopping
from one foot to the other in his excitement. For a moment,
Stu stood still, confused, trying to figure out why Cody's
ankle was suddenly better. "I thought you twisted your ankle?" he asked.

"It wasn't so bad after all," Cody said. "It's fine now."

Stu stared blankly at Cody for a moment, then the truth
seemed to dawn on him. "You were faking!" he exclaimed.

"Maybe," Cody shrugged with a sheepish smile.

"Why? Why would you do that for me?"

"Because it was your turn to score."

"Thanks a lot, Cody," Stu said. "I owe you one."

"It was nothing," Cody replied. The two boys shook hands
and patted each other on the shoulder.

Then Coach Brackett threaded his way through the throng
of celebrating players. When he reached Stu, he hugged him
and lifted him high into the air. "I'm really proud of you,
son!" he said. "You came through for us."

Cody looked up at Stu, who was beaming. He was glad
he'd made the decision he had.

More parents and friends rushed the ice to congratulate
the players. Cody's mom hurried to his side, an expression of
alarm on her face.

"Are you all right, Cody?"

"I'm fine, Mom. Trust me." He wriggled his right ankle in
a circle. "See?"

Ryan, Ernie, and Mitch had shoved their way to the players. They slapped Cody on the back affectionately.

"Don't worry, Mrs. Powell," Mitch said, nodding to his
video camera. "I've got it all on tape. I guess Cody's last-

minute injury wasn't as bad as it looked." He looked at Cody then, shrugging his shoulders in puzzlement.

"I'll explain later," Cody said.

His mom held him by the shoulders. "You played wonderfully, son," she said.

"You were a real hockey hero tonight," Tish blurted.

"I do have one recommendation, though," his mom added. "How about tomorrow we visit the second-hand store and buy you some equipment that fits properly?"

Cody smiled.

In the dressing room later the chaos simply increased. The Sharks players might as well have been bouncing off the walls. Music pounded out of the CD player. Pop fizzed out of shaken cans. A bucket of ice water was poured over Coach Brackett's head. It was sheer, utterly enjoyable, madness.

As the room began to finally settle down and the boys dressed to leave, Coach Brackett walked over to where Cody was getting dressed.

"That was quite a game, wasn't it?" he smiled warmly.

"Best one I've ever played in," Cody replied.

"I'm glad to hear that," the coach commented. He took a seat next to Cody on the bench.

"How's your ankle?" he asked Cody.

"A lot better," Cody replied. He made a show of rubbing the ankle with his hand, all the time avoiding Coach Brackett's eyes.

Coach Brackett leaned closer to him.

"I know what happened," he said slowly.

Cody turned then and looked up at Coach Brackett. The coach's eyes had a thoughtful expression about them.

"Stu explained everything to me," the coach continued. "Everything." With his hands he nervously twirled a puck. "What you did was really something. I guess I was a jerk not to see how hard I've been on Stu. I was forcing him to be twice as good as the other players just because he's my son."

Cody nodded. Stu hadn't had to tell Coach Brackett anything, Cody knew. He could have let his father go on thinking Cody had actually injured his ankle. That Stu's last-second opportunity had been a mere coincidence. But he had chosen to come clean with his father. Cody admired that.

"Stu's a good guy," Cody said. "And a good hockey player."

"I know," Coach Brackett nodded his head. "More than ever." He put the puck back into his pants pocket. "Thanks."

Cody stood up and drew up the zipper on his duffel bag.

"We can give you a ride home, Cody," Coach Brackett offered, rising to his feet. "I'll just be a few minutes with the scorekeeper and the league convenor."

"No, it's OK," Cody replied. "My mom's here tonight."

"All right, then. See you the day after Boxing Day for the regular season opener." The coach headed to the dressing room doorway, where Stu was waiting for him.

"Yeah, see you," Cody called out. His gaze met Stu's and the boys shared a smile. Cody felt relieved. Playing on the Transcona Sharks had turned out way better than he ever could have imagined. Now he was looking forward to the next game. The Christmas holidays wouldn't be so bad after all, he thought.

Cody arranged his duffel bag over his shoulder and walked out of the dressing room, replaying in his mind the highlights of the game. Not only had he scored a goal tonight, he'd also found a way to help Stu make his father notice him. As he made his way in the night to the bustling arena parking lot to meet his mom and Tish, he felt a tingle of excitement dart through his chest. He couldn't wait to get home and help them put up the Christmas tree.

16

A Second Chance

Is that about right?" Cody asked. He'd just finished wrapping a string of lights around the Christmas tree.

Tish shook her head. "Not quite," she insisted. She was wearing her brother's Transcona Sharks hockey jersey over her blouse. "Why don't you move that middle row down a bit so the lights aren't so bunched up?"

Cody unclasped some of the lights from the tree and rearranged them on a lower branch. "How's that?"

Tish made a clicking sound with her tongue. "Not quite." She took a few steps to her right to afford herself a different view of the tree.

"Mom!" Cody whined. "I'm tired from the game, and Tish is liable to have me stand here all day."

"Oh, come on, Cody," his mom cut him off. "It was your idea to put up the tree tonight."

"Yeah," Tish put in. "Let's do this right."

"You're just lucky I'm in such a good mood," Cody offered.

"I guess I am," Tish answered back, smiling.

Just then the phone in the kitchen rang, and Cody and Tish bolted from the living room. Cody had a feeling one of the guys was calling him to ask for details about the victory over the Marauders.

"I got it!" Tish called out.

"It's for me!" Cody shouted, racing to reach the phone before Tish. But her lithe body squeezed in past him through the kitchen door and her outstretched hand nabbed the phone a split second before his.

"Hello!" she panted into the phone. With her elbows she was trying to fend off Cody's hands, which were grabbing for the receiver.

"Dad!"

Cody stopped his grabbing. He thought for a second of leaving the room but decided that he wanted to hear what Tish and his dad would talk about.

"Of course I'm still coming," Tish blurted. "Mom's already arranged my ticket."

For a moment Cody had to admit that he envied his sister's trip to visit their dad in Kamloops.

"We just came back from Cody's hockey game," Tish went on. "You should have seen him — he was fantastic!"

Cody couldn't help wondering then what his dad would have thought if he'd been able to watch him play that night. He'd probably have been proud of him, he decided.

"Cody even scored a goal." Tish's face was animated. "He skated all over the ice, past every player on the other team, and then he took that puck and he whacked it right through the goalie's pads!"

"That's not what happened!" Cody cried. "You're getting it all wrong."

Tish turned to Cody. "Well, you tell him, then." She handed the phone to Cody. Without thinking, he pulled the receiver to his mouth.

"It was on a power play," he began, "and there was a face-off in the other team's end."

"You play forward, right, Cody?" his dad put in.

"Yeah, left wing." Cody answered.

"Your coach knows his hockey, then. With your stickhandling ability, you're a natural on the wing."

Puffed with pride now, Cody continued, caught up in recreating his goal, not even considering that this was the first time in months that he had really talked to his dad, the way they used to.

"Our centre won the face-off and passed back to the defenceman at the point. He slipped a pass to me and I charged the net, then passed to another forward."

"That's what makes a power play work," his dad offered. "You have to keep passing until the short-handed team finally cracks."

"The other forward, Stu, took the shot," Cody continued. "But the goalie made the save. Somehow the rebound ended up on my stick and I redirected the puck into the net."

"Good for you," Cody's dad congratulated him. "The best goal scorers have a nose for a loose puck."

"Thanks," Cody said. It felt good talking hockey again with his dad.

Then for a moment there was silence on the line.

"I wish I had been there," Cody's dad said. "I'm sorry," — he paused a second, clearing his throat — "I really am, that I wasn't."

Cody was about to say, just out of reflex, "It's OK," but then he didn't, because that wouldn't be true. It wasn't OK, as far as he was concerned, not at all, that his dad wasn't there to watch him play hockey for the Transcona Sharks. It was hard, and it was tough, and Cody didn't like it at all. But he understood now that that was the way it was going to be and he'd just have to make the best of it, the same way his dad was trying to do, the same way his mom was trying to do, too.

"I'm sorry," his dad said again.

"I understand," Cody answered back.

Again there was an awkward silence on the line. In that time Cody thought about Stu and Coach Brackett, and about himself and his own dad, and he knew that his dad would never have put him through what Coach Brackett had put Stu through.

"Dad?" Cody called out, reaching out to his father across the long-distance phone line. "Do you still want to see me after Christmas?"

"Of course," his dad answered.

"I think I'll be coming down with Tish then," Cody said. "I don't want her travelling alone on the train." Cody looked at Tish then, and he could see her biting her tongue to hold back a squeal of delight. By then his mom had moved next to Tish, holding her tight, her face seeming to hold back a storm of emotion.

"I think that's a great idea," his dad said.

"I guess I'm coming, then," Cody said.

Cody thought of the games he'd miss with the Transcona Sharks while he was away in Kamloops, and how he'd have to call Coach Brackett to explain, and about how much he'd miss his mom, and even his friends. But this was something he now wanted to do more than anything else. His dad deserved a second chance.

"I hope you have a good time while you're here," Cody's dad said.

"I hope I do, too," he told his dad. He handed the phone to his mother so she could make the final arrangements, and he and Tish returned to the living room to decorate the Christmas tree.

17

Back on the Rink

"Mom, can I go meet the boys for a little while?" Cody asked. It was the morning of Boxing Day. Cody had just finished taking out the garbage — mostly wrapping paper and flattened cardboard boxes — and was standing at the back door entrance. Tish was in the bedroom deciding what she was going to wear on the trip to Kamloops.

"But you have to be ready to leave for the train station in less than three hours," his mom reminded him.

"I know, but that still leaves me plenty of time to play a little hockey."

"Hockey!" his mother yelped. "Now? You've got to be kidding."

"I'm not kidding at all." Cody grinned. He slung his skates over his shoulder and grabbed his stick. "The boys are waiting for me at the rink. We want to get one last game in before I have to leave."

At that moment Tish stepped towards Cody and his mom. She was wearing a white dress with a huge red bow tied around her waist. "What do you think?" she asked, twirling so that the dress billowed.

Cody's mom placed the palm of her hand under her chin and shook her head, a faint smile on her lips. "Tish, don't you think you'd be more comfortable wearing a pair of jeans on the train?"

"But I like this dress, Mom," Tish insisted.

"Let her wear the dress if it makes her happy, Mom," Cody put in. He took a closer look at Tish. "She looks beautiful."

Mom's smile turned to a chuckle. "You're right. She does."

"Thanks," Tish said. She curtsied.

"Can I go now?" Cody asked again.

"Yes," his mom replied. She moved then and took both her children in her arms. She hugged them tightly and kissed them both on the forehead. "You guys have no idea how much I'm going to miss you," she said. She took a puff from the cigarette she was holding in her left hand.

"Mom," Cody commented, "I thought you said you had quit smoking."

Cody's mom blew a spiral of smoke out of her nose. "I decided to put it off until New Year's," she snickered. "But, believe me, it'll be tops on my list of New Year's resolutions."

Cody laughed. "Bye, Mom," he said. Then he stood up and opened the door. He looked back at Tish. "I'll see you in a bit," he said, winking.

When Cody reached the rink, Ryan, Mitch, and Ernie were already there. It was a balmy day, with little wind and plenty of sunshine. The boys were skating around, taking practice shots against the boards.

"Hurry up, Cody," Mitch called. "Let's get this game started."

Cody chortled. Over the last few days he'd found out that the boys were crazier about hockey than ever. The four of them had played together again on the outdoor rink every day, including Christmas afternoon, since the game last week against the Marauders.

Cody skated onto the ice. Free of equipment, except his skates, stick, and glove, he sailed over the ice like a bird taking flight. The cool air against his cheeks felt exhilarating.

He closed his eyes. For this moment at least, he thought, there are no problems, no pressures.

The boys set up their rink, dragging the garbage cans into place. As always, Cody paired with Mitch and Ernie with Ryan. Once again Ryan was wearing the equipment he had loaned to Cody.

The face-off. Once, twice, three times, Cody and Ryan knocked their sticks together. Cody reached for the free puck. Mitch edged forward, expecting the inevitable pass. But Ryan protected the puck with his body. Cleverly, he slipped it behind his skates to Ernie. Cody dug his skates into the ice and began to accelerate. But Ryan stood firm at the centre line and stonewalled him. Cody fell to the ice.

"That was an illegal hip check," Cody claimed, still seated on the ice.

"I don't see any referee blowing his whistle," Ryan teased. "Anyhow, hockey's a physical game."

The two boys laughed.

Meanwhile, Ernie waddled ahead in his skates, ankles sticking out at a crazy angle, to pick up the puck. Was he ever a sight! Cody thought. But somehow Ernie managed to gain ground and soon enough he was upon the puck and moving with it towards the empty goal.

Cody pushed himself off the ice and took up the chase. Already it was obvious that Ernie was soon going to lose his balance. Cody leaned forward to steal the puck. But Ernie made one final push with his ankles and his skates glided forward. He leaned down and made the shot. Cody watched the puck as it rolled on its side through the garbage cans. At the same instant, Ernie's skates slipped from under him and he went crashing into the boards.

"One nothing for us!" Ernie exclaimed.

"Not for long!" Cody called back. This is fun, he thought.

Another face-off. This time, Cody chipped at Ryan's stick until he'd won possession of the puck. Then he swung wide to the left and sped towards the opposing net. With a quick stickhandling move that would have done a magician proud, he deked around Ernie and headed for the net, Mitch far to his right.

The net was wide open for Cody's shot, but at the last second he turned and fired a pass across to Mitch. Mitch one-timed the puck into the net.

"Not even Jeremy passes to me on a break like that," Mitch joked. "I guess I have to take back what I said about you being a puck-hog."

"The score's one to one now," Cody announced to Ernie. "And I have to be getting home soon. Next goal wins, OK?"

"You've got it," Ernie answered.

The boys lined up for yet another face-off.

But it was never to be. At just that moment, the boys heard a car pulling up to the rink. They turned their heads to see better. "That's Coach Brackett's car," Cody pointed out. The doors slammed and the trunk opened and closed. Soon there was the crunching sound of boots on gravel. Coach Brackett and Stu were walking towards the rink. Each carried a pair of skates and a hockey stick.

"Hi, boys," Coach Brackett called. He was wearing jeans and a light leather jacket. He and Stu sat down next to each other to put on their skates. "Out for a little morning hockey?"

"Yeah," Cody answered.

"So are we," the coach replied. "It can get awful stuffy playing in an indoor arena all the time."

Cody couldn't help laughing to himself.

"Hi there," Stu said to the boys. "How's it going?"

"Great," the four boys answered in unison.

Two nights after the Marauders game, the four boys had gathered at Ryan's house to watch Mitch's video, and Cody had explained how he'd faked the ankle injury to give Stu the chance to play left wing. The boys had agreed that, considering the circumstances between Stu and his dad, Cody had done the right thing.

"We're not breaking up a game of yours, are we?" the coach asked, directing the question to Cody.

"No," Cody smiled. "I was just helping to train these guys for next year. I think they might be trying out for the Transcona Sharks, too."

"Good for you, boys," the coach said.

Ryan, Mitch, and Ernie looked at each other, and then at Cody. They couldn't help breaking out in a fit of cackles.

"We're done now, anyhow," Cody said then. He turned to Stu. "See you in a few weeks," he said.

"Yeah, see you," Stu answered back. "We'll sure miss you on the Sharks. You're really important to this team. As long as you keep that right ankle strong, that is."

"Yeah, right," Cody grinned. "Don't worry, I'll be back."

"I'll keep the left wing spot warm for you," Stu joked.

"I'm sure you will," Cody said.

By now Stu had laced up his skates and stepped onto the rink. His dad followed him.

The boys stepped off the ice. But they remained a moment behind the boards to watch Coach Brackett and Stu. The two of them glided across the ice in loose circles, their legs pumping easily, their sticks sweeping ahead of them. In time, as they crossed from one end of the rink to the other, they began passing the puck back and forth. The only sound in the morning air was the slap of the hard black puck against first one stick and then the other.

Then a train coming to a crossing blasted its horn, and the boys turned to see it cut across the white expanse of snow-covered field behind the rink.

The four boys turned to leave. Behind them, father and son continued passing the puck between them on the outdoor rink.

"I guess I won't be seeing you guys for a while," Cody said his friends. It was time for him to make his way home. Tish and his mom would be waiting anxiously.

"Have a good trip," Ryan said.

"Have fun," Ernie added.

"And don't forget to bring back a souvenir," Mitch put in.

The boys patted him on the back and then took off. They would probably go hang out at "the Igloo" for a while, Cody thought. He pushed on ahead, switching his stick from one shoulder to the other.

Now his mind was filled with thoughts of Kamloops. He was looking forward to seeing his dad again. He couldn't help wondering if his dad had been able to buy him what he had requested for Christmas over the phone a few days ago. A brand new pair of hockey gloves. The old ones his dad had given him really had become too worn and battered. Maybe they do belong in a museum, Cody thought, smiling to himself. Or should that be the Hockey Hall of Fame?